It Could Have Been Love

by

Evadeen Brickwood

Episode 3

IT COULD HAVE BEEN LOVE

"It Could Have Been Love"

This book was first published in paperback by
Evadeen Brickwood on KDP Amazon

Find this book in digital format also at:
Kindle Store, Smashwords, Neobooks and Tolino

First edition 2021 by Evadeen Brickwood on KDP Amazon

Amazon Print ASIN: B08YCXPHSP
Amazon ISBN: 9798576856091
NLSA ISBN: 9781049206189

Cover Design by Birgit Böttner
Image Source: Pixabay
Book Layout: Birgit Böttner
Marketing: Alphalogic International

Charlie Proudfoot would rather not get involved in solving murders, but her friend Lerato Gwala, a private detective from Johannesburg, believes that Charlie's talent of intuition will give her murder investigations the edge. So Charlie agrees to help Lerato with just one more case.

In this Episode:

A young woman from a wealthy family is found hanging from a tree in a popular Johannesburg park. Her death causes a public outcry. Not only is this the third suspected femicide in a month, but Candace Sedibe was also pregnant.

What role does the owner of the online dating website SugarDaddyDateMe play? Then our two sleuths discover that there can be a dark side to the glamorous sugar baby lifestyle.

<u>Other Titles by Evadeen Brickwood</u>

In the time travel youth series:

"Children of the Moon" ("Remember the Future 1")

"The Speaking Stone of Caradoc" ("Remember the Future 2")

"The Secret of the Bird God" ("Remember the Future 3")

in the German Edition:

"Kinder des Mondes" ("Erinnerung an die Zukunft 1")

Novels:

"A Half Moon Adventure" (An Adventure Mystery)

"Abenteuer Halbmond" (German Edition)

"Singing Lizards" (A Mystery-Adventure set in Africa)

"Singende Eidechsen" (German edition)

"The Rhino Whisperer" (A Crime Mystery)

"Der Nashorn Flüsterer" (German edition)

<u>Other Titles by Evadeen Brickwood</u>

In the Charlie Proudfoot series so far:

1) A Hazy Shade of Murder

2) Claws Out

Special Thanks and Acknowledgements

Many thanks to my late husband Peter, who patiently brainstormed the idea of this series with me, Cobus Griesel for lending his technical know-how, and my editor and beta readers for their constructive efforts in picking up pesky errors in the manuscript, especially Elizabeth Lemmon, Davina Gottschalk and Melesia Tully.

For Tshegofatso

IT COULD HAVE BEEN LOVE

Chapter ONE

A gentle wind played with her long shiny hair, brushing against the inclined face. Fine features and immaculate brown skin showed how well she took care of herself. But something was amiss.

The young, beautiful woman was not her usual bubbly self. Her face was framed by dark, synthetic locks that had slipped only a little to one side. This lovely face looked somewhat distorted with the tongue sticking out between her perfect lips.

A subtle scent lingered on the woman's soft skin, but it was tinged with an eerie insipid colour the layer of makeup couldn't hide and the sparkle had left her astonished eyes.

She wore a loose silk dress that reached the top of her knees. The fabric, still damp from a brief drizzle an hour ago, clung to her body and one of the limp sleeves was ripped at the shoulder seam. The muted colours of the designer dress blended into the background of the park, showing off her pregnancy in a subtle way. The woman had good taste. Hands and fingernails had seen a manicure only a couple of days ago - visibly a regular routine. The well-formed legs swung softly to the left and to the right, bare toes pointing to the grass nearly touching the dewy green, nails painted in a cheerful cherry red.

She had no longer moved as her slender neck was strung up with a rope, strong enough not to fray or snap. Frantic hands that had fumbled the rope into a clumsy knot, were no longer pulling on her limbs, her clothes, lifting her up until the deed was done.

Now there she was - swinging in the slight breeze by her neck, surrounded by the morning peace and early bird song. It was undeniable that this young woman had left behind a life in the lap of luxury.

Early sunbeams slid over the grassy slope and set fine dewdrops alight, not quite reaching the young woman's body. School children, domestic workers and joggers passed the tree in the park, but nobody realised that today, they were walking along the familiar copse of trees with a heavy load hanging from one of the low, sturdy branches. Not for long.

"Aarghhh! Aarghhh!" A cyclist with earphones plugged into her cold ears, got the fright of her life when she looked up and almost landed in the ditch between the wet lawn and the damp tar of the footpath. She had been listening to upbeat rhythms, urging her on along the uneven path.

The only exercise she would get today until it was time to ride home again. The woman sat up and took her helmet off, earphones dangling around her neck.

"Are you alright?"

A middle-aged man in exercise slacks jogged up to the woman, who still stared at the body hanging from the branch while rubbing her leg. She did not give him an answer. Instead, she pointed to the scene that had frightened her. A group of walkers stopped dead in their tracks and followed the cyclist's terrified gaze. A domestic worker stood nearby, staring alarmed in the same direction.

"There, there…" The cyclist cried now in a trembling voice that fast gained in strength. "Call the police! Somebody call the police!"

The domestic worker gave a piercing scream. "Oi, oi we are all going to die, we are all going to die!"

She started chattering to two men in blue boiler suits on their way to work. They shook their heads in stunned disbelief and couldn't avert their eyes. They had seen many dead bodies, but this sight came as a shock even to them.

"God have mercy!" The middle-aged man cried. He roused himself.

"Who has a phone? Who has a phone?"

"Tilly is already speaking to the patrol car," a fellow runner informed him.

"I called my security company!" Another woman waved her cell phone around. "Poor girl! Looks pregnant. Oh how horrible!" She wiped a tear from her eye.

"I don't want to see this. I'm going!" Her friend said in a shrill voice. She turned around and stumbled a few steps towards the parking lot, only to double over and retch into the bushes on the other side of the path.

Two girls in prim school uniforms stared at her in disgust and walked past the growing group, the older one pulling the younger girl along by the straps of her satchel. They noticed a thin face topped with dirty dreadlocks gawping at the scene from behind some shrubs. The eyes quickly gazed at them, which urged the girls on to walk even faster.

Nobody else saw the hobo in his dark rags in the spot, where he had spent the night like so many other nights before.

He had awoken from a fitful sleep to an ugly scene. The drizzle hadn't bothered him, but the noises that caught his attention were too strange in the quiet park. He wished it had been the usual security patrol searching the bushes with their torchlights.

Anything but this. For a fleeting moment, the notion of calling one of the security guards had crossed his mind. Then he had thought better of it. The hobo wanted nothing to do with all that.

His life was difficult enough even without a murder happening right in front of his rheumy eyes. After it was over, he'd seen the gold ring with the pretty green stone on the beautiful girl's finger.

He knew he'd never be able to sell the ring, not for what it was worth. But it was pretty. He'd gently slipped the ring off the lifeless finger. Surely, the girl was no longer in need of such a fine piece of jewellery.

Not even when he'd still had his job at the petrol station - and a girlfriend to buy pretty things for - had he owned something so beautiful. The ring burned like fire in his grubby hand in the pocket as he watched the schoolchildren walking by quickly.

Sirens were blaring in the distance. They came closer. The police were on their way to the scene of the crime. The hobo moved back into the undergrowth, picked up his damp blanket and disappeared as so often, unseen.

*

'Do you have all your liquids packed properly? Only in 100 ml see-through bottles in your hand luggage!'

'Yes I know, sis. Mom's on my case all the time. Everything else is in the suitcase. I'm taking only toothpaste and moisturiser in the hand luggage.'

Leleti pulled a face and Mrs. Morake waved at her in the background. 'Hi, darling! Don't worry, everything's under control here.'

She waved at Charlie and walked into another room to inspect her youngest daughter's luggage one last time. She walked past behind Leleti's back with a stack of neatly folded tops, putting her finger on her lips to let Charlie know that this was an intervention.

Charlie Proudfoot was on a video call with her 16-year-old sister in New York. She couldn't wait to see her. Leleti was coming to South Africa for a 3-week visit! And, of course, she thought she was all grown up.

'Charlie, I must go now. I still have to go to the hairdresser. I'll send you a message from the airport tonight. Did you get the flight number and arrival time?'

'Yes, I did: Thursday 23rd, arrival time 19:06, flight number XLT348.'

'Yup, that's it.' The teenager grinned broadly.

'Be careful when you are at the airport. Also in Dubai. Don't talk to strangers. I'll be there waiting for you in the arrival zone. Remember, it's a big area when you come out through the glass doors, I'll be to the left. In the front. And don't forget that it's cold here now. Put on a cardigan or a jacket before you disembark.'

'Sure... I will be careful and I'll remember to wear something warm. Thanks for reminding me 150 times, at least. I've been there before, you know. And I'm travelling with Emma, remember? You're as bad as Daddy. If it was possible, he'd come with me in my handbag. Mom also keeps telling me to take the summer tops out of the suitcase…'

'Mhm.' Charlie didn't let on what she'd witnessed just a few moments ago. 'They only mean well. You're our baby, you know.'

'Whatever. Are you coming with Jono?'

'I hope so, Leti. Jono bought a new car, now that he's got this job. So he'll be the one driving to the airport. Okay, I'll let you go now. Get a simple hairstyle please, or people will think you're Beyoncé.'

Leleti Morake laughed. 'Don't worry.' Their mother was calling something from the other room. 'Yeah mom, I'm coming,' Leleti called back. 'She's saying goodbye to you. Love you, Charlie!'

'Love you too, Kleintjie!' The screen went dark.

Charlie Proudfoot sighed deeply. The dogs were barking outside and she heard Jono yell. "Come, come. Popcorn, come here. Inside, inside!"

The new neighbours were on the street, laughing and shouting. Charlie heard a car start and hoot goodbye. They could be so annoying!

"What is it about these people? They are living

half their lives outside in the street," Charlie said as Jono came up the steps and walked into the kitchen.

"Hi there, talking to yourself again?" Jono smirked.

"Hey watch it! Show some respect for your little sister." She smiled and switched the kettle on. "Tea?"

"Sure, thanks. I never know if you are talking to yourself or to some dead person that popped in for a visit."

"Okay, touché! But somebody is coming to visit tomorrow…"

"Leti? Is she coming tomorrow already?"

"Hey, don't tell me you forgot. We have to be at the airport at six tomorrow night."

"No problem. Have to take 'The Bread' out for a bit of a drive in any case."

Jono's car was a spacious station wagon and he'd named it immediately for its compact shape.

"We just video-called and I gave her a few last-minute travel tips." She poured the boiling water over the tea bags.

Jono took the cup from Charlie. "I'm sure she just loved that. Mom and Dad are giving her an earful of tips already." Jono got himself the milk from the fridge. "I remember those days when I shipped out to Palo Alto for the first time. Mom gave me a whole list of instructions."

"You were the first one to fly the coop," Charlie grinned. "She didn't sleep the whole night until she got word of your safe landing."

"Leti is flying on her own for the first time. I understand the fuss, but she's responsible for her age. So everybody just calm down."

"So she says, but you can never be too careful. She is only sixteen."

"She may only be sixteen, but I wouldn't be surprised if she was already dating." Jono sipped his tea and looked at Charlie over the rim of his cup.

"What? Don't say that. She is so young," Charlie said in a flustered tone.

"When did you start dating?" Jono asked her slowly.

"I don't remember exactly." Charlie quickly drank from her cup.

"Oh really? I do. You were sixteen. Justin… forgot his last name."

Jono sat down on a kitchen chair and Popcorn lay down on top of his feet with Billie snuggling up to him.

"You got me there. Justin Trefoil. Yeah well… big love, but never went further than a French kiss." Charlie Proudfoot said.

"Yuck! Do I really need to know stuff like that?"

"You started it. So there!"

"Right." Jono hung his head in shame and they both laughed.

"We have to keep an eye on Leti then, I guess. She'll be staying with Emma's grandparents' for a few days. Apparently, the parents are in Cape Town on some business trip."

"No problem, I'm on it. Okay, gotta work now. See you later sis."

Jono picked up his cell phone.

"You're so lucky you can work from home for that software company."

"I know, much better than having to go to an office every day."

The dogs pricked their little ears, when an old motor car stuttered noisily outside in the street, followed by a series of revving sounds. Only one car made such a noise in the morning.

The hairdresser's husband was leaving for work in

his ancient mini-cooper.

"No barking!" Charlie said sternly and the dogs settled back down. "I'm sure the neighbours are loving this noise in the morning."

"Wow, look at this!" Jono was holding up his cell phone.

"What is it?" Charlie looked worried.

"A new post in the area's Facebook group. They found a woman hanging from a tree in the park." Jono appeared to be reading the comments.

"Oh no… in *our* park?" She asked and tried to catch a glimpse of the post.

"No, Emmarentia Dam."

"When was that? Do they know who she is?"

"Wait, too many questions at the same time. Let me see. She was young and… apparently pregnant. This lady here, Angie, says she looked so pretty even in death. She was busy jogging in the morning when she saw her. Police are working on it."

"Bummer, pregnant - really?"

"Yes, sorry, I shouldn't have mentioned it." He looked up. Charlie Proudfoot had lost her baby at 5 months in a car accident in New York that had also claimed her husband. Jono knew that his sister still grieved her loss.

"It's alright," Charlie sighed and put her hand on his arm. "Poor girl. I wonder what happened. Maybe she was depressed."

"Or somebody killed her. Gender-based violence maybe? It seems to be getting worse by the year. They found another dead woman next to the Golden Highway last week and a young girl in the field not far from her house."

"Yes, it's a damn scourge in South Africa. Beginning of last month it was the boyfriend, who choked his girlfriend to death, then was caught when he tried to burn her body. Then two weeks ago they found the remains of an art student, who had gone missing last year. Under a new cement slab, stabbed by some cookoo relative. People are up in arms about the murders."

"I know, it's awful. That makes already four this month that we know of."

"But this one… I'm not so sure about it, Jono."

"What, are you getting vibes or something?" Jono asked. He was used to his sister's dreams and bouts of clairvoyance.

"I don't know what to call it… it's probably nothing."

"It's always something with you," Jono said and opened the kitchen gate. "Wanna talk about it?"

"Nay. Go and work. Somebody's gotta earn the bacon around here."

*

In the afternoon, Lerato called. "Guess what?"

"The girl they found hanging from a tree at Emmarentia Dam?" Charlie guessed.

"Sho, you're good!" Lerato sounded impressed. "How did you know that?"

"Jono saw a post on Facebook about it. I just put two and two together, that's all."

"Yeah, I bet. Well in short, the father of the woman phoned me just now. Wealthy family in Bryanston, lots of dough. Girl went missing couple of weeks or so after Easter. He wants us to take the case."

"That's a few months back. Did you say us? You mean you and Andy?" Andy was Lerato's partner in the Maitirelo Private Investigation Agency. "Are you okay to work on a murder case again? What does the therapist say?"

Lerato had been abducted together with her boyfriend Peter Munirwa during her last investigation. A murder in the Kruger Park of a zoologist with a local university that had gotten out of hand. She'd been seeing a psychologist for the past three weeks.

Peter had quit the counselling sessions after the first week, because of a work commitment, but Lerato had stuck with it.

"No, by *us* I mean *you and me*. And – before you ask - I've got the all-clear from Dr. Smyth. The whole thing taught me to be more careful next time around. Andy works in the background in any case; he's been back at work for a month now. Mother and baby are thriving, but he's working only part-time. Just to make sure everything is going smoothly at home. Florence is a great help, though. She still checks things for us online. Love her to bits."

"Good, I'm glad to hear it, girl! I had no dreams or anything about your victim, so I don't know how I can help. All I know is that she was young and pregnant. Sorry, Lerato."

"But I need you to help me with this case, Charlie, any way you can!"

"Come on, are you serious? I have an interview at 2 o'clock…"

"For a job? Can't you postpone it? Wayward husbands and fraud cases I can handle by myself, but when it comes to murder…" Lerato sounded anxious.

"Postpone it? I need to earn some money again, Lerato. Bills don't pay themselves."

"Doesn't Jono have a job now?" Lerato asked in an innocent voice.

"Yes, but I also need to work." Charlie sighed.

"Don't you roll your eyes at me, young lady!"

"How can you possibly know that? Are you psychic?" Charlie joked. She was alluding to the fact that Lerato Gwala wanted her friend involved because of her 'intuition'. Of course, Lerato thought that Charlie had psychic abilities with ghosts popping up all the time when they were working a case.

"I wish!" Lerato chuckled. "Tell you what: I still have to do a few things this morning. Other cases… paperwork, but how about I'll give you a lift to the interview and we have our meeting straight after over coffee? Then you can decide what you'd rather do."

"Oh, I don't know. Can you be on time? The

offices are in Randburg, so you need to be here at least half an hour before the interview. If you let me down, you can forget about me working with you ever again."

"I'll be there at 1:30 sharp," Lerato promised.

She didn't make it on time and Jono had to drive a disgruntled Charlie to her appointment. At least, Lerato had left her a voicemail.

'I'm so, so sorry! This client held me up. He didn't believe that his wife we were tailing isn't sleeping with the neighbour. Thought we were lying and didn't want to pay the remainder of the fees he'd agreed to. Of course, Andy left early and wasn't there to help. It took me half an hour to convince the guy. Please, please give me another chance.'

When she got home, Charlie was in a better than expected mood, because the interview had gone really well. The pharmaceutical company was delighted with her and the HR lady said they would call about a second interview.

"I'll let it slide this time, but you'll have to come around to the house if you still want a meeting. Jono had to go out and I don't have a car yet."

"Right, I'll be there in 10. Let's go to the Magic Cuppa in Linden. We can talk there."

"Alright. You have 10 minutes." Charlie hung up. Why not? The least she could do was hear her friend out.

She dressed in casual clothes. Jeans and shirt were more appropriate for a coffee shop than a pantsuit and silk blouse.

This time, Lerato arrived early and the dogs yapped in excitement when she knocked on the main gate. Charlie slipped on her second shoe, grabbed her handbag and rushed out the door.

"You didn't have to come so early," she said as she unlocked the gate.

Lerato had jumped out of the car and took Charlie's bag. "Here, let me. Didn't want to take a chance and you never know with traffic." She was obviously sorry.

"Well, if you put it like that…" Charlie locked the gate and they drove to the nearby coffee shop in Linden.

They discussed the case of the young woman in the park over cappuccinos. The dead woman's name was Candace Sedibe, and her father was loaded. Lerato shared all the details she had been given up to this point by Marius Vorster, the homicide inspector in charge. She'd talk to the Sedibes in the morning.

Charlie Proudfoot paged through the initial police report and looked at the photographs. Not a nice sight, but then these crime scene photos never were.

"Is Marius working with us again?"

Inspector Marius Vorster had been assigned to assist the Maitirelo Agency in their last high-profile case and the collaboration had proved quite successful.

"He wasn't sure, but he'll help us, of course, if necessary. As usual, his department has more than enough cases," Lerato informed her. "By the way, he asked about you."

"He did?" Charlie frowned at a photograph that showed the ripped seam of a silky designer sleeve. "Strange that she doesn't have any bruises on her, yet her dress is ripped. Has the cause of death been established yet?"

"The coroner is still busy with the body. The morgue was inundated this morning. Some fatal dispute between taxi operators. Three dead. One's a bigwig taxi boss. That case took preference, but I'm sure the victim's father, Walter Sedibe, will pull some strings to speed things up. He's got connections."

"Do we have to go to the mortuary?"

"Yes, I do. But you don't have to go if it upsets you too much."

"No, it's okay. I'll go with you. I need to see for myself. Poor kid."

"Yeah, it's tragic. Apparently, there was some boyfriend in the background. An older guy. And since she went missing after Easter, there is a chance that she stayed with him. Name's Eugene something… Eugene Matthews. Rich… owns an online dating site and whatnot. The relationship with her parents was not great. They didn't even report her missing and she didn't contact them. Candace's mother was more upset when she heard about the pregnancy than her death."

"That's an unusual reaction. Maybe they were fighting."

"Possibly. She's her stepmother. There are four siblings. An older son from her previous marriage and the younger two are with Mr. Sedibe."

"How old's the victim?" Charlie asked.

"It's in the report."

"Ah yes, she was twenty. Not too young, but

young enough for a *blesser*. Did she live at home –
before she disappeared?"

Blessers were sugar daddies. That's what they
were called in South Africa.

"She stayed in the guest cottage at the back of the
property. The younger siblings, a brother and a sister,
live in the main house. Not a bad living arrangement,
so something else must have been up. The older
stepbrother is 22 and studies in Grahamstown. He comes
home only for the holidays. Posh family home."

"In Bryanston?" Charlie wanted to know.

"Riverclub. I thought we should go and see the
coroner first tomorrow morning. Maybe Sedibe can
pull some strings to hurry things along. Then we can
go and see her family."

"You're the boss, Lerato. I'll just tag along."

"Does that mean you're on board with the case?"
Lerato probed.

"Well, at least for now. I'm going for a second
interview soon, so I don't know yet how that'll pan
out. We can take it from there."

Chapter TWO

"No, we didn't find any visible bruising. Still checking for deeper bruising and injuries, though. Suspected suicide at this stage. I'm guessing the foetus is around five to six months..."

The chief coroner was a young dark-haired man by the name of Jonas Meyerson. He had a habit of pushing his spectacles up on top of his head as he answered Lerato's questions.

His serious expression would suddenly crack with bouts of cheerfulness. It gave him a bit of a crazy-nerd appearance, but Lerato had known Jonas for a while and wasn't bothered by it. Dr. Meyerson wore a large blood-spattered apron that had seen a good number of autopsies today.

He walked over to the metal basin that was mounted against the wall and meticulously washed his hands, before slathering on hand sanitiser. Two other coroners walked past them, discussing some document. They inspected Lerato's enviable figure before leaving the gloomy dissection room through the rubber-flap door.

A pasty-looking Candace Sedibe lay stretched out on top of one of the mortuary slabs.

Not far from the name tag that was tied around her left big toe, was a small butterfly tattoo. The forlorn tattoo added an almost childlike note to her tragic state.

A rounded shape pushed up against the white sheet that covered most of her body. Charlie stared at Candace Sedibe with pity, seeing something, the others could not see.

"Conception would coincide with her time she went missing, then. We'll have to find out who the father is. Can you do a DNA test, Jonas?"

"We can do that, but it will take a few days. We're up to our eyeballs."

"Yes, I understand. As long as you can give us a preliminary report so long."

"Will do. I don't get many cases like this one." The coroner scratched his head. "We've had quite a few murders of young women this month."

"So it might not be suicide, then?" Charlie asked.

"I can't say for sure, but suicide is always a strong possibility in a situation like this. Even more so, if we don't find bruising or defensive wounds."

"I suppose… but then there is the ripped sleeve on the dress," Lerato said.

The coroner sounded almost bored. "All I can say is that she was probably alive when the hanging occurred."

"Poor thing, but that doesn't really tell us much. We'll patiently wait for your verdict on the suicide issue. Can I have the report by tomorrow morning?" Lerato pushed Dr. Meyerson into a commitment.

"Are you also on my case now? The commissioner is already breathing down my neck. Must be friends with the Sedibe family. I should have known that this is another high-profile case. Oh joy, will have to work overtime again, then. At this rate, I'll never find a girlfriend. The taxi feud murders have been taking up all my time yesterday."

"Sorry, Jonas, but I'm also under pressure here." Lerato sighed.

"What else is new?" The coroner muttered under his breath.

"Tell me about it. What do you think, Charlie?" Lerato asked her friend, but as so often, Charlie seemed lost in thought.

"Charlie?"

"Is she the white witch?" Jonas Meyerson whispered. It seemed that Charlie had acquired a reputation after the last case.

"Could you not call her that?" Lerato whispered back then said aloud. "Charlie?"

"Emm, yes?" Charlie Proudfoot had noticed an indentation around the young woman's ring finger. That could mean that she had a partner and was possibly even married or engaged.

"Penny for your thoughts?"

"Oh nothing, just trying to let it sink in. She may have worn a ring on her finger." She smiled at the coroner and pointed to the indentation.

"Indeed. I'm sure I would have detected it sooner or later. Was just getting into it."

"Of course. We'll explore her situation," Lerato said. "Thanks for speeding things up for us…"

"Are we done here?" The coroner asked. "Sorry, but I have to get on with it."

"I guess so. Unless there is anything else, you would like to show me?"

"Nothing at this stage. As I said, I didn't quite get around to start on her. But because it's you, the forensic inquest will be ready in the morning."

"My heartfelt thanks… and the commissioner has nothing to do with it?"

"Okay, you got me there." Jonas Meyerson laughed and did a little dance. "He's expecting to hear from me as well, of course."

"That's what I thought. So I'll hear from you first thing?"

"Sure. You still owe me lunch, remember?" The coroner grinned.

"I nearly forgot," Lerato teased him. "How about this weekend?"

"You're on."

One of the other coroners came back through the flapping door and nearly bumped into them. "Oh, so sorry," he mumbled and trudged on.

The two women left the mortuary and in the parking lot, Lerato couldn't wait another minute. "So, what is it you saw in there?" She asked eagerly.

"What?" Charlie had been lost in thought again

"Come on, don't keep me on tenterhooks! Did you see the ghost of the dead girl?"

"Oh that. Actually, I did." Charlie walked on. "And the little one. In fact, there were a few around."

"Oh no… really?" Lerato was astounded. She'd been in the mortuary so many times and had never even felt a ghost. But she wasn't easily side-tracked. "What did she say to you? You were far away in your own world."

"She didn't say anything. Just showed me some jewellery, stroking some necklaces in her hand and pointed to her finger."

"That's it? Didn't she let you know what happened?" Lerato seemed disappointed.

"No, but she held up a glass with juice or something and drank it."

"Poison?"

"Possibly." Charlie shrugged.

"Alright, wait. Let me talk to Jonas." Lerato Gwala dialled the number of the chief coroner on her cell phone. "Jonas? Hi, it's me again, Lerato. Could you do a tox screen? Yes I know she was found hanging from her neck, but I have a strong suspicion that it wasn't suicide. Don't call her that! Okay, yes I know, I'm not the most patient person. Thanks, hey. Speak to you tomorrow morning."

She put the phone back into her handbag and walked towards the car.

"I knew you would come in handy." She winked at her friend.

"Gee thanks. Always glad to be of service." Charlie closed the passenger door.

"Next stop: Riverclub." Lerato started the car. "Better get out of town before traffic picks up. I hate driving here."

"Don't I know… The CBD is your favourite place. But please let's get to Riverclub alive."

"I'll do my best… come on!" Lerato was shouting at the GPS in her car. "5513 Ballyclare Drive… there it is."

'5513 Ballyclare Drive,' the GPS answered. 'In 400 meters at the roundabout, take the second exit…' the monotonous computer voice continued to give exhaustive directions to the Sedibe home in an affluent part of town.

*

The Sedibe home was everything that could be

expected in the affluent suburb of Riverclub. Charlie and Lerato were in awe when they passed a double row of tree ferns and a rough wall with water rippling down into a hidden basin as they entered the house. The whole place reeked of money.

They had been sitting with the dead woman's father and his wife for five minutes on a tasteful cream-coloured lounge suite.

"No, we didn't report her missing, because she sometimes had a boyfriend and stayed over for weeks at a time. Then Phyllis saw her when she came back to take some of her stuff out of the cottage."

The dead woman's father seemed almost angry in his response. They knew that grief could express itself in strange ways – even in anger. "We thought she would stay away just a bit longer this time."

"This time? So Candace left the house regularly for longer periods of time without telling you where she was going?" Lerato probed.

"Yes, she did." Walter Sedibe didn't seem willing to divulge more information.

"And Phyllis is your housekeeper?"

"Yes."

Her stepmother sat next to Mr. Sedibe on the luxurious couch in front of a large glass window that displayed a small courtyard covered in ferns around a trickling water feature.

She nodded in agreement. Her clothes, jewellery and hairdo showed off her wealthy status. The woman took out a tissue and dabbed it at her eyes, but Lerato didn't buy it. Mrs. Sedibe didn't seem to be close to her stepdaughter.

"Candace is… was… always so headstrong; so demanding," her husband said. "My wife had her hands full with her… whims. I have to work long hours and I'm often away on business trips to be able to pay for all this…"

Walter Sedibe waved his arm around in a grandiose gesture, showing off the open-plan living area, while his wife nodded and sniffled into a paper tissue.

The property was undeniably upmarket. Not only the house itself but also the park-like garden with a large bespoke swimming pool, waterfalls and slide in the front. But that was not a good-enough excuse to neglect one's children.

… and we have three other children, clamouring for

my wife's attention. Two of them are still in school here. Thando, my wife's son, stays in res at Rhodes University. He was home for Easter…. Candace was supposed to go and study as well this year. I paid her tuition for the Business College in January, in advance, but apparently, she only went there for two weeks and I didn't have the time to check up on her. So ungrateful. I mean at twenty she should be responsible enough to know what's right and wrong."

Visibly troubled, he jumped up to walk up and down between the couch and the floor-to-ceiling window that displayed the small courtyard.

"Did she come back home at any stage after she took off - this time?"

"Not while I was here, but I believe that my wife saw her leaving with two Louis Vuitton cases she got for Christmas. There was an Uber waiting outside. Wasn't it, Edna?"

He turned to his sniffling wife, She nodded without answering and dabbed her eyes. Lerato turned to Mr. Sedibe again.

"And you say that her boyfriend at the time was a certain Eugene Matthews? Did you assume that she moved in with him?"

"Pah boyfriend!" The two PIs looked up in surprise. It was the first thing, Mrs. Sedibe had said since they had started their interview.

"Oh, wasn't Eugene Matthews Candace's boyfriend?"

"A sugar daddy, that's what he is! She wanted to make money, make it on her own. Selling herself to someone like that." The woman flared up, only to deflate again when her husband glared at her. There was a palpable dissonance between the spouses.

"Edna, she's dead. At least show some respect for the dead."

"A sugar daddy?" Lerato looked at her friend. She was doing all the talking, while Charlie tried to feel out the situation. They had discussed this in the car earlier and so far, it was clear that there was more to it than the wealthy couple let on.

"Excuse me, could I use your bathroom, please?" Charlie stood up.

"Ah yes… you can use the downstairs toilet. Through there. Phyllis will show you the way." Mr. Sedibe made a dismissive gesture towards the maid, who had been waiting in the background by the impressive marble staircase for orders to take or fetch more coffee.

"What do you think happened?" Charlie Proudfoot asked Phyllis, the maid.

"I don't know, but Candace was not a happy child," Phyllis said in a sad tone.

"Oh? What was wrong with her?"

"You mustn't tell the Master that I said so, but he didn't give Candace attention, since her mother died. He had this girlfriend, then that girlfriend, until he married that one over there." Her tone was full of contempt. "And her son…" Phyllis clucked her tongue in disapproval.

"I see. So she looked for love with older boyfriends like Mr. Matthews?"

"I don't know him. But she was looking for love elsewhere, yes."

"Are you a police?" A little voice asked and Charlie turned around. A young girl of about 5 years was hugging the doorframe to a playroom. She looked up at Charlie unsure if she was allowed to do this.

"Nana, daddy said you must stay in your room," the

maid reprimanded the little girl. "Your mom won't be happy." There was fear in the girl's eyes.

Charlie squatted down to speak to the girl at eye-level. "No, I'm not from the police. I'm just a consultant. We are trying to find out what happened to your sister."

A slightly older boy appeared behind the little girl. "Is Candace really dead?" He asked. Obviously, nobody had sat the children down to explain.

"I'm so sorry," Charlie said slowly, at a loss what else to tell them.

"Chris, Jennifer!" You must go to your rooms now until mama calls you," the maid said sternly. The children said goodbye to Charlie and obediently disappeared into their rooms. Phyllis gave a deep sigh and walked on.

"They don't seem so happy either. Didn't their parents talk to them about what happened?" Charlie asked.

The maid walked tensely ahead without answering her question. She was either done talking or worried about repercussions if the children talked.

Charlie followed Phyllis to the guest toilet,

thanked her and locked the door from the inside.

"Okay, what's going on here?" She whispered to the tacit spectre sitting on the toilet lid and tried to make sense of the rapid gestures that followed.

*

"I can't put my finger on it, but something's not right with that family. I mean they seem to have plenty of money and all that, but none of them seems happy." Lerato sighed as she pulled out of the property. "They weren't telling us the whole truth. Not even the housekeeper, as far as I can tell."

"She's afraid. Especially of Mrs. Sedibe," Charlie explained.

"I noticed that. Why didn't they let us speak to the children? Children often tell the truth without realising it." Lerato gave another frustrated sigh. "How am I supposed to find out the truth if not even my client gives me what I need."

"He's firmly under his wife's thumb."

"Clearly, she's not as cut up about Candace as she wants us to think."

"Clearly. She gave us a few hints. It's not exactly unusual for a neglected kid to look for love in all the wrong places. Sugar daddies exploit that, of course. Just shows you that money is no guarantee for happiness."

"You'd need a psychiatrist to make sense of what's going on in that home. A narcissistic stepmother can drive anyone around the bend."

Lerato drove over the tenth speed bump along the curvy road. "Damn is this supposed to make a neighbourhood more secure by breaking my car? Anyway, step-mom seems angry with Candace even now. And Mr. Sedibe… well, talk about superficial. I suspect that he looked the other way. Emotionally unavailable."

"By the way, I spoke to her," Charlie threw in casually.

"You did what?" Lerato forgot to slow down before the next speed bump. "For goodness sakes!" She groaned. "You mean you spoke to Candace?"

"She showed me what you've already figured out. And that she feels sad for her young siblings. Her older brother is not her favourite, either. But seems confused."

"Really?" Lerato's jaw dropped. "Is that becoming

a habit with you? Ghosts?"

"Speed bump," Charlie said.

"Right." Lerato took her foot off the gas pedal and onto the brakes. This time the car slid over the bump smoothly. "Are we still going the right way?"

The GPS wasn't talking for some reason and Charlie had to give the directions while studying the screen.

"Yes, turn right down there. No, the next one… then take the third road to the left by a small shopping centre."

"Sooo? What did the victim say?" Lerato asked impatiently.

"She didn't exactly say anything. She was just a fuzzy shape, but I knew it was her. She'd been hanging around in the big reception room."

"And?"

"I understand that it wasn't a happy home for her. Her stepmother put a wedge between everyone and her older brother got all the attention. She was engaged and thought she'd found love with someone."

"Eugene Matthews?"

"Probably."

"And she told you all that while we were at the

Sedibe house?" Lerato stepped on the brake again just before the shopping centre. They were on their way to Eugene Matthews' house.

"Turn left here. Then it's three roundabouts and somewhere to the right." Charlie instructed her. "Yes, when I went to the toilet. I needed some peace and quiet. Candace didn't actually say anything, but she communicated it to me."

"I'm not even going to ask…" Lerato turned the steering wheel and zoomed through an amber traffic light.

Charlie pondered her encounter for a minute. "I wouldn't be able to explain it."

Lerato studied the house numbers to the right.

Most properties in this area had been developed into townhouse complexes with grandiose names like Magnolia Court or Hillview Estate. Not many could afford a mansion or townhouse in this area.

"Hmm. So in other words, her boyfriend was her fiancé?" She asked.

"At least that's what I understand."

"Boy, are her parents out of the loop or what! Well, we'll find out soon enough. All we have to do is ask Mr. Matthews directly. Didn't she tell you, who murdered her?"

"Again…no. I don't think she knows yet. That's why she's helping us the way she does... and she doesn't really speak to me."

"That would have been too easy. Tell her thanks all the same."

"I'm sure she can hear you. Second driveway to the right. No. 127."

"She can hear me? Now that's creepy… phew, I nearly drove past. Goodness, look at that entrance! That's one grand mansion - and of course, he has his own security guard!" If the Sedibe could be topped, it was this place.

A uniformed man studied them through a window from the small guard house by the wrought-iron gate. Lerato stopped the car in front of the large gate.

She rolled down the car window and the guard bent down to speak to her. "Is Mr. Matthews expecting you?" He asked.

"He should. I phoned him earlier to make an appointment. My name is Lerato Gwala from the Maitirelo Agency and this is my associate Ms

Proudfoot."

The guard handed her a short form to fill in and spoke into his walkie-talkie. "Alright," he said and the large gate swung open. He pointed up the driveway to the left. "You can park your car over there."

"Thank you." Lerato steered the car up the paved driveway, around a faux-Tuscan fountain and parked between a silver Mercedes Benz and a Landrover. "That was a business-like welcome. One could think we're at an office park or something."

The mansion had three levels with terraces and large glass fronts. A swimming pool sparkled farther down the lawn. A flustered housekeeper rushed outside from an invisible back door to greet them.

"Good day, ladies. My name is Bertha Lekota. Mr. Matthews is waiting for you on the first floor," she said slightly out of breath. Obviously, Mr. Matthews hadn't told her that he was expecting visitors and she had interrupted some task to meet the guests.

"Nice crib," Charlie said and looked around.

"Yes madam, very nice. Mr. Matthews is upstairs. He is by the smaller pool," the somewhat stern woman answered and led the way to the first floor.

"Smaller pool," Charlie repeated under her breath and whistled softly.

The mansion was tastefully decorated in a modern style, studded with some period pieces and art objects in between.

"Is this a Pierneef painting?" Lerato asked the woman. She referred to a painting that was mounted on the feature wall facing the staircase. They climbed the last steps and Lerato checked the signature just above the bottom edge.

"Yes, madam, it is," Bertha, the housekeeper, said on a sigh.

"Very nice. I thought I recognised the style. "

"Do you love art?" Bertha Lekota asked Lerato tetchily. Charlie didn't follow their conversation and she thought the painting rather boring.

"Not really, but Pierneef was an acquaintance of my late grandfather's. They often worked together." Lerato moved up to the last step.

"I see." The stern housekeeper tried to hide her surprise.

Jacobus Pierneef was a very famous South African

painter and she wondered if she'd underestimated the young private detective, who didn't strike her as particularly sophisticated.

Charlie seemed to pay attention to everything but the artwork around her while holding on to the polished handrail. She had detected a slight shimmer at the bottom of the stairs and knew what it meant.

In the living room upstairs, the tiled floors were covered in thick Persian carpets and slatted shutters were letting in just the right amount of light through the floor-to-ceiling windows.

Bertha walked ahead through the spacious living area to the open glass doors that led to an outdoor deck.

Two beautiful young women were splashing around in the swimming pool. They leaned against the tiled edge and chatted to a third topless woman, who was lying tummy down on a deck chair under a big sun umbrella.

As Lerato and Charlie followed the housekeeper through the sliding doors, a silver fox, possibly in his fifties, greeted them with a broad smile.

The mature playboy wasn't bad-looking for his age, tanned and fit and very casual. Thankfully, he was wearing shorts and a sports shirt.

"Ah, my dear ladies. Welcome to my place," he said charmingly to Charlie and Lerato before he addressed his four companions. "Girls… make yourselves scarce, please. Mavis will put together some snacks for you in the kitchen."

The women obediently pulled themselves up on the edge of the pool and assembled dripping wet around his lounger. The topless woman rolled over, holding her bikini top up and fastened it on the back, before slipping on a see-through kaftan. It didn't do much to hide her assets.

"I can't eat now. I have a figure to maintain," she pouted and swept her blonde extensions back with a languid gesture, planting a kiss on the man's prominent forehead.

"Mavis doesn't seem to like us, Eugene," the redhead complained and the other bikini-clad ladies chimed in.

"This morning, Bertha told her to be polite to me," the third one said. "All I wanted was coffee with vegan milk and she was so, so grumpy about it."

"She always gives me the evil eye." The beauty in

the see-through kaftan grinned.

"Then put something decent on, Yolanda. Mavis is just a little old-fashioned."

Eugene Matthews sat up and gave the redhead a playful slap on the ample backside, before the women filed into the house, muttering and giggling, followed by a stern-looking Bertha Lekota.

So, that's what sugar babies look like, Charlie thought. They seemed to her like a bunch of self-conscious playboy bunnies. Not that she's ever met any.

"Please have a seat," their host said and pointed to two deck chairs close to his lounger. "Would you like something to drink? I think we still have some leftover Perrier and ice tea here somewhere."

"No thank you, Mr. Matthews. You know why we are here, don't you?" Lerato said and took a seat.

"Yes of course, because of poor little Candace. You are the private detectives, her father hired. It's so sad. She was my favourite girlfriend." He seemed less distraught by her demise than could be expected under the circumstances. "Pity that I never met her family. Her father must be struggling to pay for your services."

"Not really. Girlfriend? I thought you were engaged to her."

"Engaged? Who told you that? You mean, because she was pregnant and lived here with me? I gave her a ring, that's true, but I wouldn't call that an engagement. It was more like a promise ring." He shrugged casually.

"Promise ring?" The two sleuths looked at each other.

"Yes, that's what I would call it. If I like a girl, I give her jewellery and sometimes it's a promise ring."

"What kind of a promise would that be?" Lerato couldn't help sounding a bit sarcastic.

"Oh, just that I care about her and that she's important to me. That's all."

"Could she have misunderstood your gesture?"

A tall empty glass on the edge of the swimming pool shattered with a loud chink. They stared at the glass fragments.

"That was odd…" Eugene Matthews marvelled. "Must be the sunlight… hotter than I thought… strange. Ah well."

"Yes, it must be the hot sunlight," Charlie Proudfoot said in a slightly sarcastic tone and grinned. She knew better.

Lerato shot her a warning glance.

"Things like that do happen, Mr. Matthews," she said and moved on from her unanswered question. "What exactly is it you are doing for a living?" Lerato couldn't be distracted by whatever Charlie was seeing right now.

"I run a dating website. SugarDaddyDateMe. Well, I own it and my computer guy runs it. You've probably heard about the app." Pride resonated in his voice.

"No, I haven't," Charlie said truthfully and shrugged.

"Neither have I," Lerato pressed on. "And, if you don't mind my asking, are you dating all of these ladies here? Do they all have promise rings?"

"God no! They are just part of the family and are here to console me. Poor little Candace. It was such a shock to all of us! I took the girl in a week or so after Easter, when she came to me crying. Pregnant she said but didn't want to tell me, who the father was. I hadn't seen her since Christmas, so it wasn't me."

"What made her so special to you that she *deserved* a promise ring?" Charlie asked.

"She was so pretty and refined. Always beautifully

turned out and educated. Astonishing when you consider her background..."

"Her background?" Charlie mumbled under her breath then said aloud: "So you were not the father of her child?"

Chapter THREE

"Good lord. I know better than to knock somebody up in this business." Eugene Matthews snorted contemptuously.

"And what business would that be?"

"Well, I'm bringing lonely people together through my dating website. It's a niche business," he explained. "I broker the transaction between men, who have made their mark in the world and don't know how to spend their money, and young, beautiful women, who appreciate a contribution to their income - and won't say no to the luxuries such a man can provide. To pay for their studies mostly. What can I say - I'm a people person. " He knew it was a hard-sell and gave the two sleuths a winning smile.

"And Candace was such a beautiful young woman in the market for a wealthy man?" Lerato probed.

"Yes, she was, and quite popular, too."

"What's *your* role in this lucrative… transaction?" Lerato asked.

"I play fairy godmother - or godfather - if you like. Once in a while, I throw a party here at the house. Let's call it a Meet and Greet, where interested parties can make each other's acquaintance. Only the men pay an entrance fee, but I assure you they don't mind."

"I'm sure they can afford it, too. And what are *you* getting out of it?"

"Got to have some fun now and again and not just work, work, work all the time," the businessman groaned.

"Yes, the word work springs to mind." Eugene Matthews missed the sarcasm in Charlie's voice. "It sounds an awful lot like prostitution." When she saw Lerato's glance, she added quickly, "if you don't mind my saying so."

"Oh no, you got the wrong idea, young lady. There is no sexual payback required… if both parties are in the mood, then why not," he chuckled. "We are all adults, but it's definitely not a requirement. I offer them companionship - completely above board. It's mostly things like escorting a gentleman to dinner or a business function or such – as arm candy if you like.

I don't blame you for thinking otherwise. Many people do."

"I'm sure they do." Lerato cleared her throat.

"Yes, you see, Babsie for example. She is studying towards a degree in Marketing and Yolanda…" Lerato interrupted his flow of words.

"Did Candace tell you at any stage, who the father of her child was?" The sugar daddy shrugged his shoulders.

"I'm afraid, she never parted with this bit of information and I didn't press her on the subject. I mean it was her own business, and who wants to talk about such serious issues, anyway? We were doing everything we could to make Candy comfortable here. I still don't understand why she felt the need to end it all."

"It's our job to find out, sir," Lerato said.

"I'm sure you'll find out soon enough if you're worth your salt." He chuckled again. "And what are DNA tests for?"

Charlie felt revulsion for this shallow playboy, who made his money by exploiting needy young women. She tried to figure out if he was telling the truth about his relationship with Candace Sedibe. *Would a fiancé behave like that? Possibly...*

"The coroner is conducting tests," Lerato said." A number of men will be asked to give a DNA sample. Only then might we know more. Are you willing to participate?"

"Sure, you can have my sample right now," Eugene Matthews said in a slightly provocative tone. "But I'm telling you, it's not mine."

"I understand. We'll get back to you on that, shortly."

He grinned. "As you wish."

"Mr. Matthews, how did you and Candace meet?" Lerato continued with her questions and the web millionaire leaned back on his lounger.

"Through the website. She'd applied on the app and her profile hit the spot. She was invited to one of my private parties and boom... we hit it off after she met her initial suitor. Well, after we parted amicably, I found her another companion."

"When was the party?"

" In... wait... April of last year, I think."

"So you'd known Miss Sedibe for about one year before she moved into your mansion. Is that right?"

"Yes, about a year. In fact, I think it was the party before Easter that year. Many of the girls showed up in bunny costumes."

"How would you describe your relationship with her?" Lerato asked.

"We were intimate… had a brief fling, if that's what you mean."

"Umm, yes that's what I was getting at. What were your plans for her after the child was born?"

"I would have helped her stand on her own feet. We can't really have babies running around this place." He lowered his voice. "Bad for business."

"Indeed. Why did you take her in, then?"

"I'd promised to care about her and I take my promises seriously." He seemed to ponder his sense of loyalty. "She said she had no place to go and that her parents had kicked her out of the shed in Alexandra that she shared with them. How cruel of her parents! She's trying to go to school, better herself and raise a child at the same time. What a lack of money can do to some people. Amazing how she levelled up all by herself."

"What do you mean by that?" Charlie wanted to

know.

"She always turned up in elegant clothes and perfect makeup. She was doing well for herself, escorting wealthy men and so on. Unbelievable, how she looked after herself, living in a township and all."

Lerato debated the idea of filling him in on Candace's background, then decided to continue the interview.

"But wasn't the child getting in the way of her plans, then? What wealthy man wants a pregnant woman on his arm?"

"Getting knocked up wasn't the best way to go, but she wanted to figure it out by herself. I couldn't just kick her to the kerb..."

"Excuse me, she told you that she was living in a township and that there was a lack of money at home?" Charlie piped up.

"Yes, that's what she told me. Used to work at a high-end store in Sandton while finishing school. She got her clothes and makeup cheaper as an employee. Some employee discount. Amazing how she cleaned up despite her circumstances. Educated, too..." he repeated. The man truly didn't have a clue.

"Mr. Matthews, I'm afraid there is something you

should know…" Lerato began, but Charlie didn't want to stay around when she put him straight on Candace's background.

"Excuse me, do you mind if I use your restroom?" She got up from her pool chair.

"You sound like an American. I thought I got a whiff of it from the start. Or is it Canadian? I really can't tell the difference. If you ever decide to change industries, let me know. Men here would go crazy for your type, hunn."

Eugene Matthews gave her a once-over and Charlie suddenly felt stark-naked in her modest summer dress. Had he winked at her? She felt annoyed by his sleazy remark and glared at him, ready to take that arrogant man down a notch. Then she thought better of it and decided to play along for the sake of their investigation.

"Ah yes, the dating site. Must be a worthwhile business. I always wanted to be a sugar baby as a side hustle and could do with the extra cash for sure. Still paying back my student loan. What's the site called again?" She was surprised at how easy it was to lie to the man. Lerato seemed as surprised as she was.

"SugarDaddyDateMe, darling. Check out the app. You'd fit right in. Lots of millionaires are looking for pleasant company. Quality men, who are lonely and don't mind spoiling a girl. Why don't you come to my little get-together next weekend?"

"Sure, why not," Charlie said lightly. "Thank you, Mr. Matthews."

"Call me Eugene…"

"Thank you, Eugene." Charlie fluttered her eyelids at him.

"And you too, of course, Miss…" The playboy businessman said graciously.

"Gwala," Lerato sighed.

"Miss Gwala. We have something for everyone. Turn around for me…"

"I will most certainly not!" Lerato said firmly and Mr. Matthews gawped at her, unused to being turned down. "And I have no time for parties. Not like my associate here." She played along and winked at Charlie. "I wish I could pay her more, but as a businessman, you know how it is."

"Don't I know," the fish was biting. "If you should ever find the time…"

"The restroom…?" Charlie came to Lerato's rescue.

"Ah yes." Eugene Matthews directed her to the guest toilet on the same floor and Charlie Proudfoot took off, leaving Lerato to set the playboy straight on the truth about Candace Sedibe.

By the stairs, she bumped into the formerly bare-breasted young woman. "Hi, I'm Charlie," she greeted her sunnily.

"Hi, I'm Yolanda." The woman didn't smile. "Just Charlie… hey? Don't think that you can wriggle *your way* into this place," she snapped before Charlie could ask her a question.

"What do you mean?" Charlie was taken aback by her hostile response.

"What do I mean? Now that the little gold digger is gone, he's of course looking for a replacement. And you can take a number for all I care."

"Okay, that's good to know… Yolanda, isn't it?"

"I'm first in line, by the way. Then come Hayley and Davina. Then nothing for a while and then Babsie. But I'm the one to look out for."

"Thanks for the heads-up. I'll keep that in mind.

Right now, I'm looking for the bathroom." Charlie had no intention of getting into an argument with the supercilious sugar baby.

"The toilet is down that passage to the left." Yolanda pointed in the general direction of the passage. She snorted and tip-toed down the stairs, her see-through kaftan fluttering about. The woman had her queen bee role down pat.

"Hmm, tough bird," Charlie mumbled to herself and looked around the carpeted living room area. This luxurious place had been home to the murdered girl. During her exchange with the not so friendly Yolanda, however, the apparition of Candace Sedibe had been strangely absent.

A part of the large room was partitioned off with wooden folding doors. The doors were open, She could see that it was a less formal TV room, complete with a large flat screen, comfortable chairs and a reddish Persian carpet. She looked over the photographs on a sideboard in the lounge and detected two framed pictures of the victim next to other photos of various people.

"Looking for something specific?" Charlie shot

around and stared at the housekeeper's inquisitive face.

"No, I just saw the photographs here and wanted to have a quick look. You are Mavis, right?" she asked. Charlie wanted to observe if her remark could put a chink in the woman's armour.

"God no, Mavis is our cook. I'm Mr. Matthews' housekeeper, Bertha Lekota." The woman said proudly, sounding somewhat like her boss. "I met you outside."

"Oh yes, of course, that's right." Charlie tried to appease the stern woman. "Sorry, I'm a bit scatter-brained today."

"Yes. I heard Yolanda speak to you out of turn." Bertha grunted. "She thinks you are competition. But of course, you are here to find out what happened to Candace."

"Yes, I am, but I suppose her behaviour comes with the territory. I was actually looking for the bathroom, but perhaps I should have a look around since I am here. Do you mind?"

"No, of course not. Anything we can do to help. It's so very sad what happened to Candace… and the baby."

"Very sad," Charlie agreed. It was surprising to her that she was getting mixed signals from Bertha

Lekota. The woman had barely stood out to her before. Where was the ghost of Candace when she needed her? Bertha showed Charlie around the first-floor living room. The TV room held a special attraction for her.

"Did Candace spent a lot of time in here?"

"Yes, she liked to sit in that green chair. The girls often watched TV series," the housekeeper explained and closed one of the open folding doors. "Would you like for me to take you to the toilet now?"

"That would be nice of you," Charlie said politely, but she couldn't shake the vague feeling she had about the woman. They walked towards the passage. "Since I'm speaking to you, would you mind answering a few questions for me, please?"

"No, I don't mind at all. If it helps to find the truth..."

"It would definitely help. I'm sure you've answered questions by the police before, but I thought we could have a bit of a chat." There was a slight glow around the uniformed woman that collided with the strange feeling Charlie was picking up.

She took it as a good sign.

"Where were you the day before yesterday?"

Charlie asked her while she walked around the room, followed closely by Bertha Lekota.

"It was my day off. Mr. Matthews had a small get-together planned. I left in the morning to visit my children in Vosloorus. They are staying with my mother. I went to the shops to buy some food before I took the bus."

"And when did you return from your visit?"

"The last bus normally arrives up the road at around 8 o'clock at night, but it ran 20 minutes late. I still had to walk home, so I must have come back at around 9 o'clock. I went straight to my room at the back."

"And there were still guests around at that time?"

"I wouldn't know. Sometimes one of the gentlemen sleeps over, but I don't think anybody was here last night." Bertha plumped up a cushion on the couch.

"Do you know who was invited to the get-together two days ago?"

"Oh, the usual crowd. Men, who like to cheat on their wives with a young woman - or men, who are looking for an airhead-girlfriend."

"Yes, that's the impression we get. Could you please give us some names?"

"I think the young ladies, who are here, can help you with that better than I could."

"Right. So they were also invited and are still here." The woman nodded.

"Where was Mr. Matthews when you returned?"

"I don't know. I didn't enter the house. Perhaps he was in bed."

"At 9 o'clock? Does he often have an early night when he throws a party?"

"I didn't say that he sleeps alone."

They had stopped in front of the open door that led to an en-suite bedroom.

"Okay, I understand. Do you remember if his car was here?"

"Which one? He has five cars. At night, they are usually parked in the garage."

"I see. Did you notice anything unusual?"

"Just that the TV was still on, here on the first floor. I could see the flicker from the driveway and heard voices. Mr. Matthews doesn't normally watch reality shows like the Kardashians, so I was surprised. Then again, some of the girls could have watched TV on their own, but I can't be sure about that."

"That would indicate that the get-together ended early. When did you notice that Candace was missing?" Charlie asked. "We don't have the time of death yet, but it's likely that she left sometime during the day."

"I suppose. When I started working this morning, the TV was off and later I saw that Candace was not in her room."

"Well, thank you very much. I'm sure that my colleague has more questions for you later." Charlie nodded and Bertha Lekota nodded back.

"With pleasure. You can use the loo in here."

Two of the young women, she had briefly met by the swimming pool, stormed noisily up the stairs with sandwich-laden plates and settled in the TV room. Yolanda, the queen bee, was not with them. They either ignored Charlie or they hadn't seen the rookie-PI and the housekeeper.

"Thank you."

Charlie walked into the room. She had seen and heard enough to form an idea of what life at the mansion was like. For now.

*

"Ah, there you are," Lerato sighed with visible relief. "At last."

She had put Eugene Matthews in the picture about the victim's true identity. That she had not grown up in a hovel in Alexandra township and that her father was, in truth, rolling in money.

His reaction had been astonishment at first. Then he'd padded himself on the shoulder for the fact that she'd run to him, the selfless benefactor, regardless. It hadn't taken him long to change the subject back to himself and his business, while she'd tried to get a clearer picture of last night's events.

His memory seemed remarkably sketchy. When Charlie joined them, Lerato sat uncomfortably on the edge of her deck chair and listened to his exploits.

"It's not a bad way to make money. So think about it…" The middle-aged playboy winked at the PI and she'd felt even more uncomfortable. Did this man ever see women as anything else than things to make money with?

"I will Mr. Matthews, I promise." Not…, she thought.

The playboy addressed Charlie. "Did you know that Candace came from a wealthy family in

Bryanston and that she attended a private school? I'm stumped."

"Yes, I did know that. Although I think she was happier with you for some reason than with her wealthy family."

"Yes, yes she was. I guess I must have done something right." He chuckled.

"Indeed," Charlie said.

"Could we please talk to the other persons here, please?" Lerato stood up and walked over to Charlie. "Especially those, who could enlighten us about what happened two days ago?"

"Certainly," the website millionaire said. "Bertha, please assemble the troops."

"Yes, Mr. Matthews," the housekeeper answered.

"Could you also give us a list of the guests, who were here last night?"

"Way ahead of you." Lerato waved her notepad in Charlie's face. "We'll confirm with the women, who attended just now."

Eugene Matthews leaned back in his deck chair and took off his shirt, revealing a hairy, muscular chest. "Of course, feel free. I'll be out here if you need me. Need to do some work. My secretary can't be expected to make decisions now, can she?"

"Thank you, sir. Which room can we use for the interviews?" Lerato asked.

"The TV room." He slipped on his sunglasses and picked up the long-drink glass from the low table next to him, before switching on his laptop. "Bertha will show you where it is."

"Thank you, sir. We'll be out of your hair in no-time." Lerato and Charlie exchanged a telling look. He waved them off and went back to enjoying the sunny day and his work commitments.

"So what did he say? Doesn't seem too cut-up about his lover's demise," Charlie said in hushed tones and looked back just a split-second to make sure that they could talk freely.

Lerato shrugged her shoulders. "Apparently, Bertha Lekota, had the day before yesterday off and he didn't see her come home. Turned in early. Of the staff, only the cook and the security guard were here. Ah yes, and the maid who comes three times a week."

"I already spoke to Bertha on my way to the restroom and she basically confirms that. She was out the whole day in Vosloorus, visiting family, and didn't come back until about 9 o'clock," Charlie reported to Lerato. "She doesn't know who the guests were but says that the TV was on when she came back, judging by the flickering she saw up here. She didn't see anybody and went to her room at the back. Bertha noticed only this morning that Candace was not in her room."

"Wow, Charlie, you're getting good at this! Who knew you could be so sly and grab the housekeeper for questioning." Lerato seemed truly impressed.

"It was more of a coincidence. One of the girls was quite rude to me and she overheard what the chickie said. Basically apologised for her behaviour."

"Rude? Why was she rude?"

"She thinks I'm competition. It seems they have no clue that I'm also investigating."

"Interesting. So they compete with each other for the prince of the world?"

"Looks like it. Perhaps we can use that to our advantage somehow. I could go undercover and check things out."

"Doesn't sound like you'd be welcome in the family."

"I can handle it."

"First, we conduct the interviews," Lerato Gwala interjected. "You could act as my assistant, take notes and so on."

"Isn't that what I'm already doing?"

Lerato's phone rang. "Hi. Yes, a couple of minutes." She walked towards the window listened. "I see… Thank you, Florence. Speak to you later."

"So, what does Florence want?"

"I asked her to check into our victim's past." Lerato whispered. "Well, it looks like our Romeo here was not her first lover. She began her sugar baby career at the age of about fifteen, even before using Matthew's website. According to her school record, the first time she bunked school for two weeks straight, she'd gone off to Durban with a Mr. Whitehurst. At fifteen. She'd told him that she was eighteen and needed money for her studies."

"Bloody hell! That's young. What happened to the guy?"

"Probation. Charges were pressed, but not much came of it. I don't know how. It's statutory rape under the law. Someone, who has sex with a child between

12 and 16, even if the kid consents to it, is guilty of statutory rape. Unless he or she's also between 12 and 16 or 17 and not more than two years older."

"How old is Mr. Whitehurst?" Charlie asked.

"My guess is he's not 17. He owns a building company in Edenvale."

"Hmm. She sounds like a handful. The man might still bear her a grudge. Did she see anyone else?"

"Florence didn't mention that. But that's not all. Whitehurst seems to have been her lover again when she was in matric until she got involved with our guy here. The police record was sealed, because of her age and family connections, but Florence has connections of her own."

"Impressive."

Bertha Lekota came towards them. "I suppose you would like to set up in the TV room for the interviews?"

"Yes, thank you, Ms Lekota," Lerato said.

"Oh ma'am, nobody calls me that. It's Bertha."

"Alright then, Bertha." The PI said something in an African language and the woman smiled. She answered briefly and both of them nodded.

"You can sit over here by the desk. Should I send them in?"

"Not all at the same time. One by one. How many are there?"

"Four. One of the girls was still asleep when you arrived."

"She slept here?"

"Nothing unusual about that. Little strumpets. Mr. Matthews is a generous man."

"I bet. I believe there are also other employees around?"

"There is Mavis, the cook, and William, the gardener and Jackson, the security guard. Nomsa is our casual maid. She comes three times a week. But she's not here today."

"I see. Let's start with you then, Bertha."

"Very well ma'am." She closed the folding door of the TV room and sat down primly opposite the small desk. "What would you like to know?"

Outside, one could hear much giggling and talking and Bertha was visibly flustered. "Excuse me for a moment, madam."

She left the TV room to shoo the young women,

who had assembled outside the folding door, to the far end of the lounge. "You'll wait here until I call you in."

"Yes, Bertha," they said obediently and continued to talk and giggle in whispering tones. She came back inside and Lerato switched her recording device on. The interview began. "Let's start with your whereabouts, Ms Lekota…"

She answered the questions conscientiously then sent in the other staff members and afterwards the young women one by one. The cook was busy with dinner preparations and her interview was moved right to the end.

The men seemed shy and gave monosyllabic answers.

William, the gardener, had also had his day off and couldn't enlighten them about the events that had led to the death of Candace Sedibe.

The security guard produced his visitors' record and they compared it against the guest list Mr. Matthews had given Lerato. There had been only three male guests. None of the men had stayed past 7 o'clock as it had been an afternoon by the pool.

Of course, nobody had seen or heard anything

suspicious. Now, all they needed was a statement from Nomsa, the maid. She didn't answer her phone but would be coming again the following day.

The sugar babies had been forthcoming.

"Last night I was out like a light. Must have fallen asleep in front of the TV…" the woman by the name of Babsie said and crossed her long legs. Her hair extensions and dark eyelashes must have cost a pretty penny as far as Lerato could tell.

"Why did you sleep until late this morning?" The sleuth asked her.

"I don't normally. Kind of unusual. Not that I'm a morning person, but I usually don't drink that much. Somebody put me in my bed. When I woke up, I was still wearing the same clothes I had on last night."

"Must have been some party," Charlie said.

"Hmm, I guess so." Babsie gave her a sly look. It was clear that she was as displeased by her presence as much as Yolanda had been.

Charlie wasn't sure if she should feel flattered or offended. Normally it was Lerato, who received attention for her sultry looks, now it was her who was treated as some sort of rival.

"Can you tell us, who you spoke to at the party?" Lerato kept questioning her.

"Well, there was Yolanda of course. Then Candace, myself and… and Davina. It was a small party. Hayley wasn't there. Candace was wearing her new designer outfit, but, of course, she's preggers. Davina was wearing a hot pink designer dress. Stunning, I'm telling you," Babsie gushed.

"How can they afford designer outfits?" Lerato asked her.

"Sugar daddies worth their salt pay for that sort of thing. I got such nice jewellery from mine just last week." She showed off her glittering earrings and necklace. "Pity it was a farewell present. Bob went back to the UK."

Lerato inspected the baubles. "Not bad. What do you have to do to earn such expensive gifts?"

"We are companions to rich and lonely men." The answer sounded rehearsed. "Sometimes, they take us out to events – the ones that are not married, of course."

"Of course."

"Bob's wife lives in the UK, so no problem there.

He took me to polo games and awards evenings, that sort of thing. We also go to restaurants or just stay in and watch Netflix. The men are very grateful for the company, I can tell you. No cheap clothes or shoes in my wardrobe. They pay for my extensions and beauty treatments. Everything. I wouldn't be driving a car if it wasn't for Bob." She casually fixed her hair. "And these babies don't come cheap."

Babsie propped up her boobs that were plainly visible under the silky dress.

"I see. And sex?"

"Sure, sometimes, but I'm not a prostitute if that's what you mean. I got into this because I need to pay for my studies."

"Nobody is saying that. Where do you find those men?"

"They usually find me. Online mostly."

"Like the SugarDaddyDateMe website?"

"Of course. There are others, but that one is pretty good. Can I go now?"

"Just now. Was Bob at the pool party yesterday?"

"Only for a short while. His flight left at 23:00. He wanted to say goodbye. A real pity. He was my regular."

"When did you see Candace last?"

"Oh, that was when we went to the TV room after the guys left. She sat over there…" Babsie pointed to the green recliner chair, in the corner.

I see. She must have been tired, being pregnant and all."

"Yeah, she wasn't hooking up with anyone these days. Eugene was good to her and Yolanda didn't like it very much."

"We heard. What do *you* think happened to Miss Sedibe?"

"To Candace? Well, I honestly don't know. Maybe she didn't know what to do, because she was pregnant and had no money. Eugene was not going to stay around and play Baby Daddy, that's for sure."

"Why are you saying that?" Lerato fished.

"I mean he's just a real nice, generous man; that's all. Well, if you like it a little rough." She chuckled then gave Lerato an embarrassed look. "Ooh, I shouldn't say things like that. I don't mind and he's not always like that."

Babsie flicked her long hair strands back. Her fingernails had little crystals glued on. Although she preferred short unadorned nails, Charlie found them fascinating. She checked if the recorder was still working. It was.

"What would you call rough?"

"Well, you know… nothing that's not legal." She backtracked. "I shouldn't have said that. It's not that bad."

Lerato put on an innocent face. "No, I don't know."

"I've already said enough. And no way would Eugene do something like that. She killed herself - right?" Babsie asked and made big eyes at her.

"We don't know yet. Thank you for your time, Miss Lowrie. Here is my card. If anything comes to mind, give me a call."

"Sure, why not." Babsie got up and traipsed back to the lounge.

The other women also divulged bits and pieces of information.

"Nomsa? I didn't see her around at the party," redhead Davina said. "But she probably was. She is usually working somewhere in the background. Mavis served snacks and kept the drinks coming. I didn't pay attention to the gardener and the guard. I chatted mostly to his one guy, Tony. He wanted to phone me later."

"Did Candace walk to the park often?" Lerato probed.

"Which park?"

"Emmarentia Dam."

"God no. Especially not now in her condition." Davina shook her head and the red locks bounced. Then she leaned back and stared intently at Lerato.

"So how did she get around – in her condition?"

"Eugene would sometimes give her a lift or she'd take an Uber to the mall if she needed something or she'd walk to the little shopping centre down the road. It's not far. For exercise, she said."

"So she didn't go to school?" Lerato wanted to know. "Business school?"

"I don't think so. She never spoke about it." Davina studied her hands.

"Don't you have classes to go to?" Lerato probed.

"We don't have to go to class every day… I'm working on an assignment."

"Why would she have left the house after the party?"

"Candace? I really don't know." The young woman looked down.

"Did Candace have reason to take her own life?" Lerato asked everyone the same question and the answers led her to the conclusion that this was not the case. Nobody could think of a viable reason why she would have committed suicide.

This meant that either it was a spontaneous decision or that it was foul play.

Next up was Hayley, who didn't have to say much since she had not been at the party, and then Yolanda strutted in. She seemed somewhat stroppy and the interview dragged on.

"Did Candace have reason to take her own life?" Lerato asked her.

"Maybe she had no money for the baby?" The young woman offered and studied the wall clock.

"What is it that you think?" Lerato asked.

"I'd say she was with her bum in the butter. Eugene would have looked after her even if it wasn't his brat." Yolanda gave Charlie a sidelong look that made Charlie's scalp tingle. *Why is Candace not here to assist me?* She thought.

"So you are saying that she didn't have a good reason to take her own life?" Lerato tried to be patient with Yolanda.

"I guess that's what I'm saying," she grumbled.

After Yolanda had left the room. the housekeeper offered the two sleuths chilled water in a jug and two glasses. She put the tray on the small desk. "You mustn't mind her. The girl's always been difficult."

"We're not here to judge," Charlie said and fumbled with the recorder.

"Thank you so much, Ms Lekota. Could you call in the cook, please? I hope she's done with her dinner preparations now. What was her name again?"

"Mavis Motseke. She's waiting outside."

"Ah yes, that's right." Lerato took a sip of her water. "Please call her in. She'll be the last witness for now. Thank you."

She pressed a button and spoke into the recorder. "Mavis Motseke, cook for Mr. Eugene Matthews, interview beginning at 14:57…"

Mavis was slight and plain and wore a preppy checked maid's uniform. She had a feisty streak but seemed nervous. Her hair was combed back into a neat bun and she wore no makeup at all. For all her simple appearance, Mavis could have been rather good-looking in her youth and when she smiled, her face lit up. Her hands were still damp from washing them before leaving the kitchen and she kept wiping them timidly on her white apron.

The death of young Candace Sedibe touched her deeply, that much was obvious. She used a corner of the apron to dab her eyes as she blubbered her answers.

"Yes ma'am, I helped with the party yesterday, until 7 o'clock. I went to my room at the back. Samuel wasn't there. Bertha, Jackson and William also have rooms in the servants' quarters."

"Who is Samuel? I don't think anybody mentioned him."

"He's my boyfriend. Samuel helps in the garden and does piece work for some of the neighbours. He sometimes stands in for Jackson at the gate. But he's been at home in Polokwane for the past two weeks. His mother died and there's much to take care of with the funeral."

Lerato nodded. She knew, of course, how important funerals were to South Africans. "I see. Tell us about Candace Sedibe. What kind of person was she?"

"She had lots of troubles ma'am. Poor girl, but rich daddy."

"You knew who she really was?" Lerato shot a look at Charlie, who raised her eyebrows. Not even Eugene Matthews had known.

"Yes. She told me her daddy was rich and lives in Bryanston, but she said not to tell anybody. Master was good to her. Not his baby, but he looked after Candace."

"Who else knew about Candace?"

"I only told Samuel," the cook dabbed her eyes. "He is quiet like a grave."

"Did she tell you, who fathered her baby?" Lerato wanted to know.

"She just cries when I ask her." The cook stared at a spot on the table and began to rub it with a corner of her tissue.

"When was the last time you saw Candace Sedibe?"

"Last night at the party. Two of the girls were arguing and Candace was crying a bit. I think they were not nice to her. Later, they sat in the TV room here. They watched Muvhango together and I made some more snacks and something to drink for them."

Mavis looked up as if she could see the scene in front of her.

"Do you know what the girls were fighting about?"

"No madam, I don't know. They often argue about stuff."

"Which one of the girls?" Lerato asked.

"I didn't see, only heard." Charlie watched Candace shake her head. The apparition sat leaning back in the green chair. Her favourite chair.

"And you didn't recognise the voices?"

"No, I did not."

She looked up to her right and Lerato could tell that the woman was not telling her the truth. "Nobody else mentioned an argument to me…"

Mavis shrugged. "I don't know."

"Can you think of any reason why Candace could have taken her own life yesterday?"

The cook didn't say anything and looked down at her hands. A tear appeared in the corner of her eye. "No, but it's not good to play around like that. They thought she had no money."

Charlie and Lerato stared at each other.

Chapter FOUR

"Who are THEY?" Lerato wanted to know.

"All of them. All of them," Mavis sobbed and focused on her hands. This didn't make much sense, so Lerato steered her in another direction.

"Did Candace tell you about the other boyfriends she had before meeting Mr. Matthews? Did she still see them?" They might be potential fathers of Candace's unborn baby, but Mavis put a damper on that line of questioning.

"No, I don't think so, but men liked Candace."

The tears were flowing again and Lerato said something soothing to her that Charlie did not understand. Her attention was drawn to a corner of the TV room in any case. The comfortable green chair. Candace, lay on the chair, hands behind her head and she appeared more defined than before.

"And you saw nothing? Candace just disappeared that night?"

"I don't know."

After a few more questions and unsatisfactory answers, Lerato let the cook go back to check on dinner. Charlie switched the voice recorder off.

"Okay, now we just need to speak to the three guests and Nomsa, the maid," Lerato stated the obvious.

"Yes, but we still don't know if it was suicide or murder. She couldn't have just beamed herself to the park. Somebody must have seen something."

"You're right. I'm not buying it that nobody knows nothing."

"That's a double-negative…"

"Oh, get off. You know what I mean." Lerato rolled her eyes and grinned.

"If it was murder, it would make more sense," Charlie said.

"Well, Jonas should get back to me soon with some information on that."

"At least we got off to some sort of a start."

"Yup."

Lerato and Charlie stepped out of the TV room and left the wooden folding door open. The housekeeper was waiting outside. "Is there anything I can do for you?" She asked in a servile tone.

"Actually yes, could we please have a look at Miss Sedibe's room?" Lerato answered.

Bertha Lekota nodded. "Certainly. Follow me, please."

"I'll stay here a bit longer and have a look around," Charlie said and Lerato followed Bertha down the passage.

Charlie knelt down and padded the carpet under the green chair. She knew what she was looking for. Her fingers touched a glass object and she picked up a shot glass with a small serviette stuck to the bottom. By the looks of it, the glass must have recently rolled under the armchair.

"That one?" The ghost nodded and applauded without making a sound.

Charlie studied the glass. It had lipstick on the rim and a greenish residue inside.

"Alright, so you fell asleep after drinking this?"

Candace nodded again and Charlie sniffed at the glass. "Smells like some health tonic. Am I right?" More nodding.

She took a picture with her cell phone and wrapped the glass and stained serviette into the tissue.

Then she dropped it into her handbag and scrambled to her feet. "One day I'll remember to use gloves and a plastic sleeve to collect evidence…"

Charlie slipped on her sandals. "But you were not the only one. Mr. Matthews also had a shot and …the other girls? Not Yolanda? What happened then?"

Candace's gaze turned to the folding door.

"Are you talking to yourself old lady?" Yolanda leaned against the doorframe and guffawed. "What are you doing there?" Charlie recovered quickly.

"I dropped an earring. Are you spying on me?"

"I live here, remember?" Yolanda smirked. "You're with the police and here I thought you were fresh talent."

"I'm not with the police. She's a PI and I have a temp job helping her with interviews. How long have you been standing there?"

"I just came in. Who were you speaking to?" She chuckled. "That's so creepy."

"If you must know… it's Candace Sedibe. She's talking to me about what happened here two nights ago." Yolanda stared in disbelief.

"Get out of here…" The ill-mannered woman

smacked her lips. "You're pulling my leg, aren't you?" She laughed uneasily and took a step back.

"Am I?" Charlie was enjoying the fleeting triumph over the insolent woman.

"You're a psychic then?"

"I told you, I help the detective with her interviews."

"Get out of here!" Yolanda repeated. "Candace's is not here. Why would you ask all these questions if she could just tell you?"

"Good question," Charlie said in a mocking tone. "Got ya!"

She saw Eugene Matthews through the large window walking up and down on the deck, talking into his cell phone, while the gardener swept the paving on the far end of the pool. Matthews waved his arm around. He seemed upset about something he was hearing.

"If you'll excuse me, I have some sleuthing to do."

"I thought you only help with interviews…" Yolanda said.

Candace grimaced and shook her head.

"She didn't like you very much, did she?" Charlie goaded her.

"Who… Candace? Did she tell you that?" Her eyes were darting around the room.

"She didn't have to."

Charlie pushed past the sugar baby and crossed the spacious living room towards the passage. She had to find Lerato. Whatever it was that upset the businessman - she didn't have a good feeling about it.

"Lerato?" She called her friend and Lerato answered from Candace's room. This was important; the shot glass she had found under Candace's armchair could wait.

The room was a decent size. It had a large bed and its own bathroom.

A few tangled plastic hangers and some clothes were scattered on the otherwise undisturbed bed and on the floor.

Babygrows with price tags still attached were stacked on a chest of drawers under the window. Two teddy bears sat side by side in a blue crib with a planet mobile attached to the topmost part.

Charlie felt that the baby, Candace had been expecting, was a boy. She herself had been pregnant with a girl more than two years ago and the thought made her sad. How she had to get rid of all the baby things in the nursery that Colin had painted in a soft pastel colour just days before. He would have been a great dad. She pulled herself together and paid attention to their case.

"Lerato, can I speak to you for a moment?"

"Just now, Charlie. Come help me figure this out."

Since the two suitcases Candace owned were neatly stored in the wardrobe and the housekeeper had no explanation for the empty hangers and crumpled-up clothes, they came to the conclusion that - given the circumstances and the competitive nature of sugar babies, they had met so far – one of them had helped herself to the dead woman's designer clothes.

Lerato and Charlie were busy studying birthday cards that were pinned to the mirror above the dresser under Bertha's watchful eye when Mr. Matthews walked into the room all flustered. He lost no time in sharing his disturbing news.

"Nomsa has been found with her skull bashed in," he informed them. "Down the road. Dogs in the neighbourhood were barking incessantly, so somebody checked and found Nomsa's body. They left her lying in the bushes outside a townhouse complex!"

"What? The maid, who was here on the day of the party?" Lerato cried.

"Oh my god, oh my god, we are all going to die!" Bertha Lekota lost her composure. "Poor Nomsa, poor Nomsa!" She wailed.

"Bertha, please!" Mr. Matthews buttoned up his shirt with one hand while holding his cell phone in the other. "Is there no end to this misfortune? I just spoke to a homicide detective. He said they would send a team."

"Let me speak to him!" Lerato wanted to get clarity on the new situation.

"He hung up." Matthews closed the last button on his shirt.

"What's his name?" Lerato demanded to know.

"I forgot, but they should be there soon to secure the crime scene down the road. I'm supposed to wait here for someone. They want to ask more questions." He shook his head. "That's all I need."

Charlie ignored his last remark. "Was the name of the detective Vorster or Phaladi?" Eugene Matthews tried to remember. "It was Phaladi… Phaladi… I'm sure of it," the playboy said. "Or something like that."

"Mr. Matthews, where exactly is the crime scene?" Lerato asked him. She thought that under the circumstances she should revert to a less familiar tone with him.

"By the Mykonos Townhouse Complex, he said. When you drive down to the gate, through the gate then go left. Unless he said Morning Glory Complex; that would be the other way…"

"Don't you want to call Johan first?" Charlie asked Lerato. "We know nothing about when or how this happened."

"Chances are that he won't be answering his phone. No, it's better if we have a look at the crime scene before some numbnuts climbs all over the evidence. Those two cases are connected somehow, I'm sure of it," Lerato said. "I need to have a look at the crime scene, the sooner the better."

"Then I'll come with you." Charlie stuck a birthday card she was still holding back onto the edge of the mirror and walked towards the door.

"Mr. Matthews, we'll probably come back later

with the police. Please make yourself available and nobody should leave the premises," Lerato told him.

"Yes, yes of course." Eugene Matthews nodded. "What choice do I have?"

"Thank you very much for your help, Ms Lekota."

Bertha Lekota had been standing quietly next to the bed only half-listening. She looked wearily at Lerato and nodded. The woman seemed very tense, but Charlie put it down to the stress of being at the centre of yet another murder case and the prospect of endless questioning yet to come.

The young women, who had been playing by the swimming pool without a care in the world, now congregated in the passage.

"What's going on, Eugene? Something happened?" Babsie piped up. "You sounded so upset." They had obviously not been eavesdropping by the pool.

"Mr. Matthews is not at liberty to speak to you right now," Lerato answered. "But it has to do with this case and it's quite possible that we will need to speak to you again, soon."

"What?" Somebody screeched. "I thought we were

free to go home."

"Not just yet, I'm afraid," Lerato Gwala said. "There has been a new development in the case. Please don't leave the property. The police are on their way."

Before they reached Lerato's car, Dr. Meyerson, the chief coroner phoned.

'What? Sorry, you're breaking up…' Lerato yelled into her phone. 'Yes, yes… I understand." She said nothing for a minute or two. "Thank you. Thanks for rushing it through, Jonas. I owe you one… I know. Speak to you later.'

She opened the car door and motioned for Charlie to get into the passenger side.

"What did he say?"

"He did the autopsy this afternoon. Not much bruising. No sexual assault, but it was definitely murder. She was already dead when somebody strung her up. He gave me a whole explanation for it. It'll be in the report. Doesn't get us closer to a motive, though. Florence is already looking into the background of Eugene Matthews and our other witnesses. Let's see if something interesting pops up." She put the car in the second gear. "They're still busy with her clothing. Negative for fingerprints or DNA, but they could see how she was held up. Don't ask me how. They're also testing the DNA profile of the foetus. That can take a while. And Jonas did a tox-screen. Here's where it becomes interesting: apparently, our pregnant victim was knocked out by a wheatgrass shot laced with nitrobenzene. Enough of the poison to cause her death. Jonas says that it's sometimes used for abortions and it's not safe. The danger of the mother dying is great."

"Shame. So somebody killed her with nitrobenzene and then made it look like suicide?" Charlie offered.

"Or… she tried to abort the child herself."

"Could it be a backstreet abortion gone wrong? But why was she hanged?"

"I don't know - and what quack would give a woman a dangerous substance like that? I guess we have our work cut out, trying to find the motive is now a priority…" Lerato said to herself as she cleared the gate. "I wonder where that poison came from. Left or right?"

"Go left."

Charlie remembered something important. "Wait… that reminds me - I picked something up in the TV room just now. Candace showed me where it had rolled under the green armchair in the TV room." Lerato stopped the car.

Charlie took out the shot glass with the greenish residue that was still wrapped into the tissue and handed it to her friend. Lerato unwrapped the glass just enough to study it for a moment.

"Of course she did," Lerato rolled her eyes. "The maid must have missed it during the clean-up. Lucky for us. Does this look like a wheatgrass shot to you?"

"Could be," Charlie said. "I imagine wheatgrass is green."

"Our first real lead. With some luck, they'll find nitrobenzene in that green goo." She covered the glass again.

"Sorry I had to use a paper tissue."

"At least you didn't touch the glass. We need to get gloves and evidence bags for you. There's plenty of room in your Mary Poppins bag, I'm sure. In case some ghost shows you evidence out of the blue next time 'round." Lerato alluded to the ghost of their last victim, a university professor.

"I guess," Charlie said. "I took a picture of it, though."

"Great. Can you send it to me?"

"Yes, ma'am!" Charlie said.

"Please hand me a sandwich bag. There's a packet in the glove compartment."

Charlie rummaged around the glove compartment. "Geez, look at that mess in here. That one?" She asked and held up a packet with sealable sandwich bags.

"Sorry. Never have time to tidy up in there," Lerato apologised. "Just take one out, so we can store the glass. No, together with the tissue. You can put it in the glove compartment for now."

Charlie placed the sandwich bag with the glass and serviette in the paper tissue carefully on top of whatever it was that Lerato kept in there, then closed it with a thud.

"Now we have another dead body on our hands. I know it's not our case, but…"

"One victim poisoned with nitrobenzene, another one beaten to death," Lerato pondered. "Why? The solution to our murder case might be under our noses."

"Do you think Nomsa was on her way to work when they jumped her?"

"Could be. I guess we'll find out just now. But she wasn't due to work today…"

"You're right. So what was she doing here? Maybe she had a piece job in the neighbourhood." Charlie offered a plausible explanation.

"No clue. It's Homicide's job to find out… We are more concerned with solving our own case. I should ask Florence to do some research on the substance. Maybe they use it at a hospital…" Lerato looked at the clock in the car. "It's a bit too late to phone her. I'll send Flo a message." She typed something on her cell phone, before phoning the lab. 'In an hour? Alright. Here's the address…'

It took Lerato no more than two minutes to organise the pickup of the evidence.

"Okay done. Now let's have a look at our poor cleaning lady." She started the car again. "You said I should go left…"

"The road looks virtually the same on both sides," Charlie observed. "But someone on the left directs traffic and there's a cluster of people on the sidewalk. Nothing of note on the right."

"Left it is," Lerato said and drove towards a growing crowd of people.

When they arrived at the scene, one side of the road was cordoned off and police officers made sure that nobody crossed the tape on the pavement.

Lerato parked in a quiet side lane and they walked back to the yellow and black tape that read 'Crime Scene – Do Not Cross'. A policewoman tried to stop them. "Sorry, ma'am, this is a crime scene. Please walk around the tape. This side over here."

Lerato whipped out her private investigator's ID and held it up for her to read.

"I'm told that inspector Phaladi is in charge of the case. I'm here to speak to him…"

"Inspector Phaladi? Yes, he's over there with the CSI team." The constable nodded and lifted the police tape for them to duck under.

She pointed with her chin to untidy bushes in front of the Mykonos Townhouse complex and stopped somebody else from crawling under the tape. "Sorry sir, please walk around the tape. This is a crime scene."

They could see the homicide inspector, who was talking to some people wearing jackets with CSI written on them. "Thank you very much, Constable," Lerato said and they walked along the paving.

"Hello. Johan," she greeted the inspector.

There was a flicker of recognition in his eyes. "Oh, good day, Miss…"

"Gwala, Lerato Gwala and this is my associate Charlie Proudfoot. We've met before… worked on the Morton case together, remember."

"Of course, I do remember now. How can I forget a beautiful face like that? I mean two beautiful faces…Sorry." The inspector nodded an apology in Charlie's direction.

"Good save. It's been just a couple of months." Charlie grinned.

"Well, we get a lot of cases in. The private detective agency, right?" Johan Phaladi addressed Lerato again. "You were the lady, who was kidnapped at the university… of course. How are you doing? Quite recovered?"

"Yes, that's me. I'm doing fine." Lerato played down the PTSD she had experienced after her harrowing experience. She couldn't let him know how difficult it was to get back on track. "A few counselling sessions and I'm as good as new." She smiled with her mouth only.

"That's good to hear, Lerato. May I call you Lerato?"

"Sure, Johan."

"What brings you guys here?"

"We were working another case down the road, when we heard about this murder," Leraro told him. "The two victims knew each other."

The inspector led the way to the bushes that could do with some pruning.

"Really. What can I tell you? Our victim was found only about an hour ago by residents. Although I don't understand why only now. Her name is Nomsa Dube, age 56." He showed them where Nomsa was still lying under a drab plastic cover. Only her shoes stuck out from under the sheet. Knock-off Louboutins.

"Different MO to our case," Lerato stated immediately. "Can I have a brief look at her?"

"Sure. Just don't touch anything."

"Hey, I'm not a rookie!" Lerato laughed.

"Just saying."

"Tony, these ladies need to see the body of our victim. They are working on a related case." His phone rang. "I must answer this," he said and walked away.

Lerato greeted the CSI technician, who wrote some information down. Somebody else was taking photos of the pavement. She squatted next to the body and lifted the plastic cover.

Nomsa Dube lay with one arm over her head, facing away from the road. Her body was completely covered from sight by the bushes. It was not a pretty sight. The woman's visible temple was encrusted with blood and tissue and some of the blood had seeped into her clothes.

"Was she killed here?" Lerato asked the CSI technician.

"I believe so. There is some blood over there…" He pointed to the pavement. "…and some closer to the kerb." There were also bloodstains on the leaves of the bushes in front of the victim.

"Enough blood in the soil to suggest that she bled

out here and wasn't moved from another crime scene," the man said. "Time of death roughly 48 hours ago."

"48 hours? That would put it in the same timeframe as our other victim. Odd that nobody had noticed the stains or the body before now."

"There's another victim?"

"Yes, poisoning case, apparently. Just got the prelim report from the coroner."

"And the two cases are connected?"

Yes, so it seems." Lerato kept talking to the technician, while Charlie Proudfoot took one look at the body. She went pale.

"Not used to the sight are you?" The CSI noticed her reaction.

"No, not to so much blood."

"Okay, go over there and take a few breaths," Lerato ordered her. "I'll finish up here. Drink some of that bottled water in your bag and don't you dare faint on me."

"Yes, mom." Charlie smiled weakly at her friend, walked away and unscrewed the cap of her water bottle. She stood on the street corner, took long, deep breaths and took a few sips of mineral water. Traffic trickled past. Drivers were rubbernecking to see what was going on, before being waved on by police officers.

"You okay?" Inspector Phaladi had finished his phone call. He knew from experience that crime scenes weren't easy on the nerves.

"Getting there." Charlie took another sip of water.

"So what case brings you to this area?"

"We're investigating another murder down the road. Victim is Candace Sedibe. We just questioned the staff at the place where she stayed. Her boyfriend, who owns some dating website, is not exactly the picture of grief. They had a complicated arrangement." Charlie waved in the direction of Eugene Matthews' mansion. "Nobody saw her leave after a party, but now we found out that it was murder."

"Really?"

"Yes, the young woman was found hanging from a tree at Emmarentia Dam yesterday morning. Her wealthy and well-connected father hired Lerato's agency to find out what happened to her. Mr. Matthews, the boyfriend of our first victim is also the employer of the lady you found here. He said you just spoke to him. That's why we came. We suspect that the two cases are connected."

"Ah yes, Mr. Matthews. He was one of the first numbers on the victim's cell phone. I heard about the young pregnant woman they found at Emmarentia this morning. Sad. I think Marius was assigned to the case. Didn't know whether it was suicide or not."

Lerato joined them. "Not. Jonas promised to get back to me speedily and he did. How lucky is that?"

"Congratulations. That's what I call a jackpot. Must be your natural charm," the inspector chuckled and gave Lerato an admiring look. "Wouldn't hurt if I had some of that."

"Don't take it to heart," Charlie said. The colour was returning to her cheeks.

"Feeling better I see." Lerato smiled at Charlie and her friend nodded.

"They are notoriously overworked at the morgue – just like we are - but since the hanging was posted all over social media, it might have spurred them on," the inspector mused. "Femicides are just out of control."

"True…" Lerato shook her head. "Connections don't hurt either."

"So did you have a good look at our victim here?"

"It looks like somebody was awfully angry at the poor thing." Lerato sighed.

"Yup, but CSI can't call it yet. Blunt force trauma to the left temple seems pretty evident, but still looking for the murder weapon. Possibly unplanned assault. Happened almost two days ago."

Lerato shrugged. "I know, your guy Tony told me. Two days in the middle of the city and nobody notices anything."

"It's been cool these past few days and no smell yet," Charlie mumbled. "They should really get a gardener to keep those plants in check."

"Mhm." The police inspector shrugged.

"Yeah, that sounds about right." Lerato grabbed the water bottle from Charlie and took a long swig. The inspector changed the subject.

"Give me a bit of a heads up on your case. I'll have to go to talk to Mr. Matthews just now and it would be better if I knew something about the other murder."

"Alright. I'm coming with you by the way. This is turning into a long day for me."

"Okay appreciated, let's collaborate. Marius is notoriously overworked. So what's the skinny on your case?"

Lerato drank some more of the water before answering. "Candace Sedibe stayed with Eugene Mattews, but apparently, he's not the father of the baby. Jonas Meyerson will test all potential sperm donors, so we are still trying to find out, who'll win the lottery. We've just come from interrogating the family in Bryanston and the people at the Matthews mansion up the road."

"Ms Proudfoot here just told me about that. Complicated, apparently…" Johan Phaladi said.

"You can say that again," Lerato continued. "Matthews is a wealthy businessman. He threw a small party the night our victim was poisoned. Still checking things out, where the substance might have come from and so on." She took another sip of water. "Nomsa Dube was also there that night and cleaned up after the party. Then she allegedly left. The housekeeper, Bertha Lekota says Nomsa always took a mini taxi on the main road up here. So she must have been on her way there."

"Candace Sedibe went missing around 8 o'clock as far as we can tell," Charlie piped up, while Lerato chugged some more of the still water. "Nobody saw her leave or remembers anything else, apart from a bit of a hissy fight by some of the women."

"Really? Sounds suspicious. Have you thought of lie detector tests?"

"We didn't get that far. Still trying to piece together the timeline. They all had a health drink after the party, so it's possible that there was something in their drinks as well. Maybe they all went to sleep and that's why they can't remember." Lerato handed the water bottle back to Charlie. "Sho, I was parched."

"Seems a bit elaborate even for murder," Charlie said.

"So there's a definite overlap. You said the coroner gave you the test results?"

"Well, not the detailed report yet, but Jonas says it was definitely murder," Lerato confirmed. "The victim was already dead before she ended up on that branch in the park. He found the poison and we also have some evidence that needs to be tested."

"Must have been some party." Johan Phaladi had seen many scenarios during his career and it still amazed him what people could do to each other.

"We didn't get much information out of the young ladies who were there, or the staff for that matter. At least now we know why our victim here didn't answer her phone today."

"So what did they have to say?"

"In a nutshell, they can't remember a thing and have no idea how Candace ended up at Emmarentia Dam."

"Hmm, that means that our victim no. 2, Nomsa Dube, was murdered roughly the same time as your victim no. 1 disappeared. Her cell phone was still in her pocket and there was some cash. 268 Rand 70 cents. Probably just got paid. That makes it more personal."

"Or some drunk lunatic attacked her and was not after her valuables," Charlie said.

"I know, shit happens, but that would be a hell of a coincidence." Johan Phaladi scratched his head. "Whoever killed her just dumped the body behind those bushes. People only became suspicious when two Rottweilers on the corner over there wouldn't stop barking. The security guard came to check and found our victim."

"They waited that long before they checked?" Charlie asked stunned.

"I know, we asked the same question. The owner says he locked the dogs up last night, and then again today because the neighbours complained."

"Great and not many pedestrians around. Still, nobody paid attention…"

"If you look at your cell phone while walking down the road, you could walk past a bag with gold coins and not notice."

"What caused the injuries?"

"No murder weapon yet and it's getting dark, but it must have been a heavy object. If we don't find anything, we'll carry on tomorrow morning. They'll have load shedding in the area in 2 hours, so no point in continuing the search now. Bloody nuisance."

"I'll say. I need electricity to work on my computer. But last night it only came back on at about midnight. Sorry, end of rant."

"I don't blame you. We can't do our job properly,

either. Wish government would get their act together," Johan Phaladi shook his head in frustration. "At least we managed to establish blunt force trauma to the skull and more or less the time of death. We did what we could do. Can you put in a good word with Jonas Meyerson for me? Maybe he's falling for your charm again."

"I can try..."

"Since you're already speaking to him… pretty please."

"Sure, I'll speak to him," Lerato said graciously.

The coroner's van arrived to take the body to the morgue. They watched how Nomsa was loaded into the vehicle on a gurney. Charlie turned away. She had seen enough.

"We should get out of here," the inspector said and called to the CSI team. "Pack it up, guys. Load shedding's in two hours."

The technicians waved and shook their heads. This was nothing new to them.

"Yes, the sooner the better." Lerato agreed. The streetlights popped on one after the other. "Oh, look at that… wonders do happen."

"For the next two hours at least. We're also still trying to get hold of Nomsa's family. Can't phone every number on her SIM card."

"I'm sure you'll get that info at the house."

Charlie tore herself away from staring at a high wall behind the police inspector, then she looked at her watch for a few seconds. "Oh my God, look at the time! I need to go with Jono to the airport. My sister and her friend are landing in an hour."

"Oh, dear. Tell Jono to come and pick you up!" Lerato said. "We can handle the witnesses at the Matthews house."

Charlie nodded and phoned her brother. 'I'm so, so sorry, Jono. This case is getting more complicated by the minute. Can you come and pick me up?' She gave him the address and hung up.

"He'll be here just now."

Good. The lab driver is coming to pick up the shot glass at the mansion in about 15 minutes. Inspector, I'll wait with my friend for a bit. You go ahead."

Johan Phaladi saluted them by tipping two fingers against his forehead and was gone.

"Anything yet?" Lerato asked Charlie in a low voice.

"Not really. I'm a bit tired of dead people, who don't want to talk to me," Charlie answered while checking the road for a glimpse of Jono's car.

"You saw Nomsa, then?"

"She was up on that wall over there, watching everything. Just a small blob of vapour."

"I didn't see anything."

"You wouldn't, but she totally ignored me." Charlie sighed. "Doesn't look like she's interested in helping us."

"Great." Lerato exhaled.

"What's our other ghost telling you?"

"Nothing. She also doesn't talk to me right now. Maybe she can't or needs more time."

A light blue car stopped at the roundabout and a young Asian man with tousled black hair waved at them.

"That was quick," Charlie marvelled. "Okay, I'm off." She picked up her bag.

"Good. Hi Jono, bye Jono," Lerato waved back at Charlie's brother. "You go and take care of your family. We'll catch up tomorrow morning."

"Good luck," she said and walked across the road.

A policeman was already trying to wave Jono on.

"And say hello to Leleti from me. If she still remembers, who I am," Lerato called, but Charlie was already explaining the situation to the impatient police constable.

Chapter FIVE

"So, are you making progress?" Jono asked his sister as he pulled off from the crime scene. "Facebook and Twitter are going bananas with speculations about the Sedibe case, and I saw a couple of newspaper headlines on the way here."

Charlie took a deep breath and put her seat belt on. "Really? I haven't had time to pay attention to the news. What are they saying?" Jono switched to the car's GPS system. *In 400 meters take the second exit…*

"As I said, everyone is speculating. Is it another femicide case? South Africa has had enough of that. Are we killing our youth? You know - that sort of thing. The police are mum about the details, which seems to make it worse."

"Well, they can't really say anything yet," Charlie explained.

"Except that it's a scandal how many women are killed in South Africa by partners. Lots of statistics.

Makes me feel like I have to protect you all the time. The people who found her in the park are giving interviews. Not sure why the police are allowing that…"

It was getting dark now, but the streetlights shone brightly on the traffic everywhere.

"Anything I should know about?"

"Somebody said they saw someone in the bushes at the tree where they found her, but that's unproven."

Charlie looked at Jono, while he tried to concentrate on the cars in front of him. Rush hour was starting to enter full-swing stage. "I doubt that whoever it was had anything to do with Candace's death."

"Oh, and why?"

"I can't put my finger on it just yet, but why would you hang around when you've just murdered someone? Plus they just found the maid, who worked at Eugene Matthews' house three times a week in the bushes down the road. Dead."

"Dead?" Jono whistled through his teeth. "I thought something was up when I drove up to the traffic circle. So many cop cars around and the policeman you spoke to didn't want me to park the

Bread, although I'd seen you standing there." He gesticulated.

"Yeah, it's been a rough day. I'm pooped." Charlie closed her eyes.

"Right. Did you have some *help* yet? You know… *from the other side?*"

"The other side?" Charlie chuckled a little with her eyes closed. "Actually, I did. I just wish she would talk to me. But Candace showed me a shot glass with green stuff in it. According to some of the witnesses, they had a wheatgrass shot last night in the TV room. The coroner found some in Candace's stomach. It was laced with some drug that's sometimes used for illegal abortions. One of the girls only woke up while we were there and can't remember what happened after the party. Neither can the others or they claim they didn't see or hear anything. Hard to tell what's the truth. Our victim just disappeared into thin air and ended up dead in the park."

"That's harsh. I mean that she was pregnant and all."

"Yes, it's hard to work with facts like that."

"Are you okay being on the case?"

"Well, I'm dealing with it, but it's not easy. She

had all that baby stuff in her room. Whoever did this committed a double murder."

"Some people on Facebook seem to think that her boyfriend did it. Others say she killed herself because she was abused and pregnant and didn't see a way out."

"Let them gossip. I don't think she poisoned herself. She seemed too confused about being dead. And either her boyfriend is a total psychopath or he's innocent…"

"How do you know that?" Jono asked her and let a delivery van in front of him.

"Hey, fishing - are we?" Charlie opened her eyes.

"No, I'm just curious." He joined the column of cars moving towards the airport. "Gee, I'm glad there are no accidents on the highway reported. There was a pile-up earlier on this route, but it seems they cleared the accident scene."

"Yeah, I'm also glad," Charlie mumbled. "By the way, her boyfriend, for lack of a better word, doesn't seem to care enough. But who knows? The maid, they found in the bushes was also definitely murdered."

"No way! And the girl died only a couple of days ago…" Jono sounded worried. "What are the odds that she was murdered by the same guy?"

"There has to be a connection somewhere, just what exactly."

"Maybe she saw something she shouldn't have," Jono speculated.

"Maybe. She doesn't want to communicate with me. Sat on this tall wall the whole time… where they found her body. At least Candace lets me know stuff that could help us, even if she doesn't talk to me. But Nomsa just sat there."

"Are you done for today?"

"Yeah, Leleti comes first. Lerato and one of the homicide inspectors are questioning witnesses as we speak, but they don't need me for that. Maybe this time somebody is going to tell the truth."

"You think they were lying earlier?"

"Of course, or not telling us what they know or suspect. Hey let's talk about something else… yeah, Leleti is coming for a visit! Can't wait to see our little one in the flesh." Charlie perked up.

"I don't like that she's staying with her friend Emma for a few days."

"Don't overreact, Jono. She stays with Emma at

her grandparents' house. Not in some dodgy hitchhiker's inn."

"Bugger. She's growing up, Charlie. It'll get difficult to keep an eye on her. Maybe I should call her often."

"That's not creepy at all…" Charlie snickered. "Your older brother checking up on you all the time, while you are trying to have fun."

"I know. Do you think three times a day is okay?"

"You can ask her when you phone tomorrow. I'll be busy with the case, so you'll have to take over in that department. Don't ask her now. She'll be tired after the long flight."

"Don't you think we should have coffee at the airport? Maybe they are hungry. It'll be late by the time we get home. Where do we drop the ladies off? Did she give you the address?" Jono asked.

"Actually, I'm not sure. Somewhere in Roodepoort. Leti will give us the address and contact details. Otherwise, they'll have to come with us…"

"Sure, even better. Really, they stay in Roodepoort? Oh, joy. That's far. I just hope there won't be any more load shedding or we'll get stuck somewhere."

"I'm sure that Emma knows the way to her grandparents' house… oh boy, looks like there's a traffic jam ahead."

"Damn, there was nothing on the news earlier."

"Must've happened just now. Take the next turn-off. We can get back onto the highway further down." Charlie sat up.

"Sure, we need to be there on time. We left rather late as it is." Jono took the turnoff and followed the new GPS directions. *Recalculate, recalculate… in 800 meters, turn left at the traffic light.*

They arrived at the airport in good time.

"Which flight number was it again?" He asked as they took the escalator from the parking to the arrival area in the main building.

Charlie pointed to the flight arrivals board. "Flight # XLT348, 19:06, New York. There it is! The plane has already landed and they are disembarking."

"On the dot. Thank goodness the flight wasn't delayed." Jono began to walk faster. They followed the signs to International Arrivals.

"Hey, are you trying to run a marathon?" Charlie

reprimanded him. She loosened the elastic that held up her ponytail and shook her hair. "Think about your poor little sister who's trying to keep up with you!"

"Sorry, sis." Jono slowed down until Charlie had caught up with him. "I'm just trying to get there before she comes through the sliding doors."

"It's still going to take a while, Jono. The passengers must first go through passport control, pick up their luggage and walk a mile to get here."

"Right…" He slowed down even more. "Will she recognise us in the crowd?"

"I told her that we'd be standing on the left-hand side when she comes out," Charlie said.

"As in HER left-hand side?" Jono asked.

Charlie laughed. "Yes, of course, dummy, as in HER left side!"

"Okay, just making sure… btw, the guy over there is totally checking you out…"

"Oh stop it! How can you even tell while racing through the airport?"

"No, really…" Jono indicated with his eyes where the offending guy was and Charlie followed his glance. "He's just standing there, staring at you."

"Please!" Charlie looked back at the man.

Jono put his arm around his sister. "Too many creeps around in a place like this."

"Don't exaggerate," Charlie said. "You're making me nervous. Is he still looking?"

"No, I think he's moved to another spot." Jono relaxed and lowered his arm.

"Good. This murder case is getting to you today…"

"Can you blame me? You are investigating someone, who murders women."

"I'll be alright," Charlie said and wanted to believe it herself.

They waited for the better part of 30 minutes and eventually, the sliding doors parted for the millionth time and their sister Leleti marched confidently out.

She had a broad grin on her face, rolling a large turquoise suitcase behind her, giggling excitedly with a blonde young girl next to her. No doubt, this was her friend Emma.

"Leti! Leti!" Charlie waved wildly to get her younger sister's attention.

"Hi, hi!" Leleti waved back and ran to Jono and

Charlie, manoeuvring the turquoise suitcase with difficulty behind her.

They hugged and she chatted about the flight and food that had been served on the planes and if she had gotten any sleep during the layover in Dubai. After some familial bantering, Leleti's friend joined them with an elderly couple.

"Hi, nice to meet you. I'm Emma and these are my grandparents." The lively girl didn't wait for Leleti to introduce her.

"Well, nice to meet you, Emma. Hello grandparents. I'm Charlie and this is Jono Morake. And this pretty young lady here is our little sister."

"Nice meeting you." The grandparents shook hands with Leleti's older brother and sister. "We saw you waiting in the front here, but I would never have guessed that you are siblings," the grandfather said.

"Yeah well, we get that a lot," Jono answered. "We didn't know you were going to be here. I was bracing myself to drive all the way out to Roodepoort."

"Well, now you won't have to. Don't worry about Leleti. She'll be safe with us."

"Oh, I'm sure of it. Should we sit down for a cup

of coffee somewhere?" Jono suggested and put his arm around Leleti's shoulders as if he was worried about his baby sister nonetheless.

"It's getting late, I think we should go back home," the grandmother said in a whiny tone and studied her husband's face.

"Yes, I think you're right, Helene. If we are lucky, we'll have street lighting on the way home, but you never know. We'd better be off."

"Oh no, that's too bad…" Charlie tried to object.

Ding, ding, ding. A flight announcement drowned out Charlie's answer.

Emma's grandfather simply took Leleti's suitcase and began walking towards the parking area downstairs. The others followed him. Leleti seemed reluctant to part with her brother and sister so soon. She took Jono's and Charlie's hands like a little girl and squeezed them.

"You still need to give us the names of Emma's grandparents, their phone number and address," Jono said. "I'll call tomorrow morning. Then we can talk properly."

Leleti blue-toothed the information to Jono's phone.

"I'll see you guys during the week, I'm sure. We can meet up tomorrow if I have nothing better to do." Emma walked up to them to say goodbye.

"Oh? If you have nothing better to do?" Jono teased Leleti. "Charlie and I need to work, but I'm sure we can make a plan. We'll talk about it tomorrow."

"Alright, but don't phone too early. We want to sleep in." The teenagers giggled.

"If the cats let us," Emma chuckled. "Summer always wants to wake me up."

"Shall we say 11:00?" Jono asked.

"Okay, 11:00 is good." The girls giggled again.

"Don't forget to phone Mom and Dad to let them know you landed safely," Charlie reminded Leleti. "I'm sure she'll be worried otherwise."

"I'll do that just now." Leleti squeezed their hands again.

"Don't forget or Mom will come down on us."

"No, I won't, Mommy no.2."

"Hey watch it Punk," Charlie laughed and the teenager snickered happily.

They hugged each other and said goodbye.

Jono and Charlie watched the grandparents totter

off with the two girls until they went down the escalator and were out of sight.

Charlie sighed deeply. "There she goes again. Stupid arrangement. Why does she have to stay with her friend for a week?"

"If that's what she wants to do… she's growing up, Charlie." Jono shrugged. "And we'll see her soon enough."

"I know," Charlie said. "Do you feel like grabbing a coffee and something to eat?"

"Hmm, you should probably eat something. Let's see if they serve low carb food somewhere."

Brother and sister sat down in one of the many restaurants at the airport and reminisced about their childhood over a plate of food.

Soon the grisly murders were at the back of Charlie's mind, but she didn't know yet what life had in store for her.

*

'He wants us to do what?' Charlie Proudfoot's jaw hit the floor. She had just learned that her second interview had fallen through and was not in the best of moods. She tried not to overthink why the company no longer wanted her for the position she'd applied for and now Lerato had sprung this invitation on her.

'Matthews wants us to come to this party tonight at his place. He calls it meet-and-greet. Apparently, you said you'd come to his next little get-together and this is it,' Lerato explained.

'Yeah, we did talk about it - sort of, I guess. But I only tried to get him off my back and because I thought it would help us to get more info from him.'

'He seems to be taking it seriously.'

'I don't even have a profile on this stupid sugar daddy app,' Charlie moaned.

'Doesn't seem to matter. You use the event for sleuthing.'

'Has this guy no sense of decency? I mean his girlfriend – or one of them – was just murdered and his maid as well. He's a major suspect and now he wants to throw another party?' Charlie still couldn't believe her ears.

Lerato didn't seem surprised at all. 'He's probably just too superficial to see anything wrong with it. In his own words: business must go on. He's just getting a few members of his dating website together and thinks he's doing us a huge favour at the same time.'

'Yeah, that's a great favour.'

'Look, it's a good opportunity for us to check out Eugene Matthews' circle of friends or whatever he calls these guys. The only problem is: I can't make it. So you'd have to go on your own,' Lerato said quickly.

'You want me to go into that snake pit on my own? You can't be serious.' Charlie grunted, but Lerato was unmoved.

'It's just one of those things. You can handle it and… just maybe… we'll get some intel or maybe… we'll even find the killer.'

'And I'm supposed to be the bait?' Charlie was still grappling with the idea of going to a sugar baby party without Lerato by her side.

'Well, not exactly - more like a representative. Of course, it can't hurt if you doll yourself up a bit.'

'Doll myself up? Lerato…'

'I'd come with you, but I need to go over the info Florence got for me and I'm waiting for test results and what not. Then there is this other case on my schedule I took it on before the Sedibe murder case popped up. It needs to be wrapped up. Jealous husband and so on.'

'Hey, I'm not your skivvy! I'm a consultant. What about Andy? Can't he attend the party as a sugar daddy?' Charlie tried to wriggle her way out of going.

'Nay, not old enough. Andy's wife has a cold and he needs to take care of things at home, with the baby and all. So he can't even do the paperwork at the office right now. Please don't let me down, hunn.'

Charlie didn't say anything for a few seconds. 'Well, if you put it that way, I guess I don't have much of a choice. Although I was looking forward to seeing Leleti later. She arrived last night.'

'Oh, of course. Sorry, I forgot. Everything hunky-dory with her?' Lerato asked.

'She's fine. The plane landed on time and it was so good to see her again, but she went home with her friend Emma. The girls are staying at Emma's grandparents' in Roodepoort for a week. That's why Jono suggested that we should meet her tonight. Lerato… she's my little sister…'

'Can't you video-call her during the day and Jono can meet with her later? It's really just for one night,'

Lerato suggested.

'I guess we could do it that way…'

Lerato sensed that she had won Charlie almost over. Just a little nudge.

'Great, it's sorted then. Hang on a sec.' She'd heard somebody at the door and walked into the front room. It was Andy, who'd come in to drop off some documents. 'I'll speak to you just now,' she said to him.

'What?' Charlie asked confused.

'I was talking to Andy. He's just popping in for a few minutes to drop something off.' Lerato motioned for Andy to wait. 'So, can I count on you?'

'Talk about twisting my arm…'

'I promise you, you won't be alone at the party. Marius Vorster will be there posing as a millionaire and he said that he'll bring somebody with him.'

'Oh, will he now? Is Marius old enough to be a sugar daddy?'

'Mhmm, yes, I think so. It's their case as well, remember? And he volunteered. You'll be much safer with a whole police escort. How does that sound?'

'Very reassuring. Can I bring Jono to the party?

I'm sure he wouldn't mind playing my bodyguard. Maybe we should meet with Leleti tomorrow…'

'Hold your horses. That kind of defeats the purpose, don't you think? The point is that single sugar babies meet potential, rich sugar daddies at this meet-and-greet.'

'Right … but the sugar babies know that I'm working with a private investigator. And what if Matthews himself is the killer?'

'You can wing it with the sugar babies and why would Matthews invite you to his party if he has sinister intentions? And if he does, I don't think he'd do anything in front of all these guests. Anyway, you even have a ghost there to protect you. But if you'd rather not go, I'll make another plan… Florence maybe…'

'Oh, that would be…'

'Sorry, Charlie, I must go.' Lerato interrupted her again. 'Speak to you later. Andy's in a hurry. I'll whatsapp you the details of the party.' Click.

"Wait… hello?" Charlie said, but Lerato had already hung up.

"Damn." Charlie wasn't too happy about the new

arrangement. "Damn!"

Billie and Popcorn charged into the room, followed by Jono, who was taking a break from analysing a complex internet problem.

"Why the long face?" Her brother asked and sat down.

"I have to work tonight. Lerato just told me that there's a party at our sugar daddy's place and that I must attend to observe what's going on. I'd much rather see Leti." She sounded rather frustrated.

"I guess work comes first," Jono said. "Any chance I could come with you?"

Charlie pushed Billie down. The little dog tried to lick her face. "No Billie, stop this," she laughed before addressing her brother. "She says it would defeat the purpose of sugar babies meeting sugar daddies if I bring an escort."

Billie and Popcorn jumped off the couch and settled under the coffee table.

"You are going as a wannabe sugar baby?" Jono exclaimed. "Get off it! Don't take it the wrong way, but aren't you a bit too old for the job?"

"Haha, very funny. I'm not exactly auditioning for

the job. The sugar daddy top dog asked for me to come. I may have played along when we saw him. He asked me if I would consider changing industries."

"No way! My sister's a sugar baby. You missed your true vocation."

"Yeah, looks like it." Charlie rolled her eyes. "And by the way, Lerato said you are too young to act as a credible sugar daddy. Marius Vorster is going to be there."

Jono whistled through his teeth. "So he's good enough, but not me? I could totally pull off a sugar daddy… IT billionaire retired young. Rich, but no talent for proper relationships."

"Sounds about right – apart from the 'rich' part." Charlie chuckled. "And didn't you say you have an online meeting just now? I'm told that it's all been arranged. I'm the sugar baby checking out the guests. Plus Marius will be protecting me better than a young wannabe billionaire, who likes young chicks and has no talent for proper relationships. He'll probably rock up with a couple of undercover cops in tow."

"You're all set then. But what if your website-guy is the killer. Have you thought of that? You might be wasting your time. And what's up with throwing a sleazy party so soon after his girlfriend is murdered - and his cleaning lady on top of it. Shouldn't he be sad or rattled or something?" Jono frowned.

"Yeah, that's what I thought, but Lerato thinks I'll be safe with the police being there undercover. It'll be a chance to get into that circle and ask a few questions. She says that he won't do anything weird with all his sleazy buddies being around."

"Playboys aren't known to be sensitive when it comes to other people. Maybe Candace Sedibe will be there and can help you a bit more this time 'round."

"Yeah, I hope so."

"Okay well, have fun. We can video-call with Leleti just now and see if she wants to get together tomorrow, instead of today. Then you can chat with her about girlie things. I'm not so good at that."

"Girlie things?"

"Yeah, you know… Look, you don't have to stay for long. If you don't feel comfortable with all those sugar daddies, I'll come and fetch you. Bugger the murder case and all that."

"Jono, have I told you that you are the best brother in the world?"

"Not lately." Jono grinned.

"Well, you are." Charlie leaned her head to the side and clapped her eyes at him.

Her brother gave her a suspicious look. "Does that lead up to the question if I can give you a ride to the party?"

"No, of course not. I'll take an Uber, but maybe you could pick me up later."

"I knew that something else was coming." Jono chuckled.

"Hey, I would do that for you, if you were invited to a sugar baby party."

"If you put it that way." They bickered back and forth for a little while. Ping.

"Wait, that's Lerato sending a message. And I totally did help you out with Amanda…. Okay, the party starts at 7 o'clock. Matthews' mansion, downstairs by the pool in the garden. The police have cordoned off the upstairs living room and the pool area, which was to be expected." Charlie put her phone onto the coffee table and Popcorn sniffed at it.

"Gee, how many pools does the guy have?" Jono asked.

"I think it's only the two, but I haven't been to the back of the house yet, so who knows." The dogs suddenly pricked their ears and charged outside. "Oh no, that must be the neighbour lady with her dogs again," Charlie sighed.

They heard wild barking and Jono looked out of the window. "I can't believe it! The old hag is hitting them again with the leash she should have on her dogs!"

The siblings ran outside, but by the time they got to the gate, the woman was strutting down the road as if butter wouldn't melt in her mouth.

"She must be senile or something," Jono huffed. "I wish they would move somewhere else. Trailer trash!"

He'd said the last few words in a loud voice, but the woman had already made it to the corner. "Oh, it makes me so mad. Why do these people try to provoke us?"

"Who knows. The dogs are okay. There's no point in picking a fight with someone like her. Come, come inside. Billie, Popcorn!"

At lunchtime, they video-called Leleti, who had

settled in at the house in Roodepoort. It didn't feel much different to face-timing with her in New York. Leleti's happy face appeared on the screen. She was wearing a swimsuit.

"Hi Leti, how do you like your first day in Joburg?" Charlie asked her.

"It's fantastic. Emma's grandparents have a swimming pool in the back garden and we've been swimming the whole morning."

"Don't overdo it. It's not quite summer yet," Jono cautioned her.

"The water is solar-heated. I'm so glad I brought two swimsuits with me. Smuggled them past Mom's watchful eye." Leleti made a face.

"Hey young lady, don't you roll your eyes at us," Charlie mocked her.

Leleti laughed. "I'm more worried about getting my hair wet, but knock on wood… so far no problem… come say hello!" She waved and Emma's face appeared on the screen, framed by wet tangled hair.

She waved to Charlie and Jono. "Hi there, how are ya?"

"We're fine, Emma. I was just telling Leleti not to

overdo the swimming. It can still get cool at this time of year."

"Ah don't worry Ms Proudfoot. It's just so great. In New York, we have no big gardens with swimming pools. Only the indoor pool in 113th Street we always go to with school, so we must make the most of it. We'll get dressed now."

Charlie decided to come out with it. "Sorry, I can't see you guys tonight. I have to work and couldn't get out of it, but Jono here is available."

"At your service, ladies," Jono said and took a mock-bow.

The girls giggled. "We can do something tomorrow. Emma and I were thinking of going out on our own. Take an Uber to West Gate and walk around."

"Oh? All grown up, are we?" Charlie said. "Mall rats even in South Africa. You're not going out with boys, are you?" There was more giggling.

"No, just window-shopping. We could meet you there at lunchtime."

"Angling for a free lunch?" Jono said sternly and the girls looked at each other.

"I mean yeah…" Leleti chuckled. "Tonight we go

to some garden party with Emma's Grandpa."

"Oh really, that sounds like fun," Charlie said. "Must be a braai. What about your Grandma, is she not coming with?"

"Ah, she wants to stay at home and watch Netflix. She doesn't go out much."

"Do you know where the party is?"

"No, we'll ask Emma's Grandpa later. He just told us it's going to be interesting and there are some girls our age."

"Leti, you better let us know where you're going or I'll come over there with my shotgun," Jono joked. "Even if there are only girls."

"Hey big brother, I can look after myself, you know. And you don't have a shotgun."

"Are you sure about that?" The girls giggled.

"Yeah..." The girls thought it was hilarious. "Maybe there are boys as well..."

"Okay, tomorrow lunchtime it is," Charlie cut in and poked Jono. "Let's not talk about boys now."

"Why do you have to work, Charlie? Do you have to do shift work at a lab again?" Leleti asked her big sister. It was the kind of work she remembered her doing back in New York.

"No, nothing like that, I'm helping a friend of mine with something. She says hi, by the way. Lerato Gwala. I think you won't remember her."

"No I don't remember a Lerato, but tell her I say hello back all the same." Leleti giggled again. "I must go. Emma is calling me..."

"Okay, off you go now and put some clothes on you."

"Alright. Love you guys!"

"Love you, Shorty!" They blew kisses before the screen froze and went dark.

"I hope the girls are not up to some nonsense," Charlie said.

"Come on, they're just going to a braai with Emma's grandfather. How bad can it be? Leleti's on holiday, so let her enjoy herself. We'll see her tomorrow for lunch, then she'll tell us all about the braai."

"You're right, I'm probably overprotective. Have you spoken to Mom at all?"

"Yeah this morning for five minutes or so," Jono answered. "She wanted to know if everything's okay.

Mom says that Leti was a bit terse last night.

"Terse? She was probably just jet-lagged."

"Yeah. Mom was busy with something and didn't have time to talk."

"Probably a surprise party for one of her friends or grading papers again. She's always busy with something." Charlie grinned.

"She handed the phone to Daniel and he told me about his studies. Halfway through his third year and busy with some exams. Daniel can be our go-to person when it comes to legal matters."

"Lol, in the States maybe, but they have a different legal system in South Africa. Is he still going steady with his girlfriend… Lilian?"

"No clue. You can ask him yourself. He's only a phone call away. Why are you making such a long face again, sis?" Jono could be quite perceptive.

"It's just… you know… that whole sugar baby scene. Imagine Leti getting sucked into something like that."

"She's got way too much sense. And why would she? It's usually girls, who are desperate to make a buck doing any kind of side hustle to stay afloat,"

Jono answered.

"Candace Sedibe wasn't desperate to make money. She was desperate for someone's love and affection. So she pretended to be poor and even that was an epic fail. That's real sad."

"Leleti doesn't need the money or has daddy issues. There was always so much love to go around at home. So don't worry yourself. And she's safely staying with her friend's grandparents, so no need to watch her like a hawk."

"I guess you're right. I'm probably too close to that murder case."

"Yeah, you probably are. I was overreacting yesterday, but I'm kind of over it. " Jono got up and the two dogs followed him to the door.

"Okay, change of subject," Charlie said and scratched her head. "It's getting late and I must turn into a sexy young thing. What am I going to wear tonight? What do sugar babies wear to a party?"

Chapter SIX

Two hours later, a transformed Charlie stepped out of the Uber taxi in front of Eugene Matthews' mansion. Dressing as a sugar baby had proven easier than expected.

She'd cinched in Jono's over-sized red t-shirt with the writing *I'm Coming For You* at the waist with a broad belt – and voilà – the t-shirt was now a sexy mini-dress. The only black heels she possessed completed the look.

Jono had helped with her hairdo as well. He'd conjured up a passable up-style and applied her makeup, all with the help of YouTube videos.

'Wow, my eyes look so much bigger now,' she'd marvelled and studied herself in the mirror. 'That's what I call talented, brother.'

'I think it's called smoky eyes,' Jono had answered. 'YouTube videos are great for that sort of thing. Some of those women were quite unattractive without makeup and look stunning afterwards. Makes for addictive watching.'

'Who knew? The video you worked with was made by a man.'

'I know. And… he did a good job. I liked his voice better. Not so shrill. Glad you like the result, sis.'

'Like it? I love it. Thanks so much, big brother! I'm shite at that sort of thing.'

'You're welcome Madam Investigator.' Jono was packing away her makeup utensils, while Charlie turned in front of the mirror.

'Totally a sugar baby. Who knew that going undercover could be fun?' She said.

'If I had to do this every day, I'd go bonkers. Not that I would ever try makeup on myself," Jono said. "Do these girls have nothing better to do than wasting their time on all that… dolling up?'

'Probably not. It's part of their 'job'. Some of the girls just escort their clients to events or restaurants and stuff like that.'

'Maybe just a few. Most of them surely have to deliver more than just being arm candy to some rich, old guy.' Jono had shaken his head.

'Probably.' She'd grabbed her purse and teetered

down the driveway to the gate, where the Uber had already been waiting.

Charlie felt a little uneasy that the driver stared at her legs and high heels. She hopped out, closed the car door and the driver took off. There were some rather larney cars parked outside the property and a security guard with a cricket bat kept an eye on them, while Jackson kept an eye on things inside.

Charlie took a mental note that circumstances must have been similar the night Candace Sedibe had been killed. Was it possible to get a body past the security guard without him noticing a thing? In a car, maybe…

"Good evening, madam," Jackson greeted her at the gate in a polite voice. "May I have your name, please?"

"It's Miss Proudfoot," Charlie said and gave him a charming smile.

The guard phoned her name through to the house, then after receiving the okay from Bertha, opened the pedestrian gate for her.

There were quite a few cars by the water feature, where Lerato had parked her red Polo the last time Charlie had been here, and even on the front lawn.

They probably belonged to the inner circle. She walked towards the thumping party music and passed two men, who were standing by the cars, smoking.

Their serious expression changed as soon as they caught sight of the stunning woman in the red mini dress, trying to stroll casually past in high heels.

"Who do we have here? I'm Coming For You. You're what I've been waiting for, honey. The evening's just begun," one of them said and took a long, seductive drag from his cigarette. Great. Charlie cursed her choice of dress, she'd thought perfect just a moment ago.

The man gave Charlie a pervasive once-over that made her feel like she needed a shower. She smiled courageously and hot-footed it past the men. The music grew louder the closer she came to the brightly lit swimming pool area.

Charlie could feel the booming of the bass drums in her stomach. People were talking and laughing, and some high-pitched voices were busy telling a hilarious story to much male laughter.

"I'm so glad you could make it, Charlie," Mr. Matthews welcomed her, his arm around a glammed-up Babsie. The sugar baby was wearing a low-cut shift dress that left no doubt about her ample curves underneath and, by the looks of it, she was the flavour-of-the-day.

Charlie was impressed that the host had remembered her name and at the same time felt sorry for Babsie. She looked so young underneath all the makeup that put her own efforts to shame.

"Thank you, Mr. Matthews. There are so many people here. You seem to have lots of fun already… and here I thought I'd come too early."

"Your timing is absolutely perfect…" he said charmingly.

"Hi Babsie. You look beautiful tonight," Charlie said.

"Thank you… weren't you here the other day with the PI? The American chick? Cleaned up nicely, I must say."

"Yeah, I'm just a temp, you know." That hadn't come out right.

She didn't know what else to say. Babsie was already tipsy and grabbed a glass of champagne from a tray that a waiter carried past them. She offered it to Charlie. "Here hunny, have something to drink."

Charlie extricated the glass gingerly from her pointy-nail tipped fingers.

"Thank you." Charlie hadn't expected the party-girl to remember her at all, but she needn't have worried.

"What?" Babsie had already forgotten what they had just spoken about.

"Thank you so much for inviting me to the party, Mr. Matthews," Charlie changed direction. "Everybody seems in a good mood."

Strangely so, she thought. Considering that two women attached to his household had tragically died just a few days ago.

"Oh why so formal, please call me Eugene." The host gulped a mouthful of beer from the bottle he was holding with his free hand. "Eat drink and be merry."

Babsie giggled. Eugene Matthews was still the middle-aged millionaire she'd met before, but he behaved more like a carefree frat boy.

"Aren't you going to introduce us, Eugene?"

The smoker, who'd used the corny pickup line in the driveway, when Charlie had walked past, stood suddenly next to them.

He looked much older now that she saw him under a bright garden lantern. The mottled skin of his face and the scalp under the sparse hair was a dead giveaway.

He lifted one eyebrow in what was supposedly an enticing gesture that made Charlie shudder.

Eugene Matthews let go of Babsie's shoulder for a moment and waved his hand about. "Introduce yourselves, kids. There are snacks on the terrace. I must go and speak to somebody over there," their host said and walked away, pulling a giggling Babsie with him.

Had he lost interest from one moment to the next? Or perhaps - he was giving Charlie a chance to do her job - sussing out the attending guests for possible clues – without having Babsie blabber about who she was.

She awkwardly eyed the rich, uncouth man; thinking of how she could best get out of the situation without having to talk baloney.

"So, your name is Charlie?" His voice was gravelly, no doubt from years of heavy smoking. Before Charlie could answer him she would regret she heard a familiar voice behind her.

"Hi Charlie, there you are!" Marius Vorster must

have seen her arrive and decided to come to her rescue. "Sorry buddy, this cutie's with me."

He put his arm around her shoulders and gave her an admiring look. The older man tipped two fingers against his forehead in greeting and walked away without introducing himself.

"Wow, was that some kind of secret code for 'this chick is taken'?"

"I'm not sure, but it worked," the homicide detective said and grinned.

"It sure did. But now, we don't know who this sugar daddy was. He never got to introduce himself to me." Marius Vorster let go of Charlie and she turned to face him.

"We'll find out some other way. I must say, you do look the part," he said with an admiring expression. "Even down to the champagne glass."

"Thank you, Marius. My brother helped me with the outfit and it didn't take a minute before somebody shoved the glass in my hand. What am I supposed to do with the champagne? I don't like alcohol…"

Marius Vorster took the champagne glass from Charlie and poured the contents on the ground.

"There, problem solved." He handed the empty glass back to her.

"Your brother helped you with that? Really? That's interesting."

"Not what you think! He just watched some YouTube videos and offered to help."

"I didn't say anything. The ladies seemed to have a soft spot for him at the WildDog event when I saw him a few months ago. That was him, right? Or do you have another brother?"

"I do have another brother, who lives with our parents in New York, but yes, Jono was with me that evening. You're right about the ladies. There was a professor, who's also from New York. She took a shine to him. Many women do, but he's fussy when it comes to dating."

The music changed to a stomping rhythm and some of the guests started to dance or sway where they stood.

"You come from a big family, Miss Proudfoot,"

"Yes, I do." Charlie surveyed the party by the pool. A good 30 guests were enjoying themselves. Mostly older men pairing up with younger women.

The only older female was Bertha Lekota, who replaced empty dishes and platters on the veranda. "Now we're at work, shall we mingle?"

"Let's go for it." They walked towards the illuminated swimming pool. A few young women frolicked in the water that seemed to be quite warm, judging by the vapour swirling over the top of the water surface. "Feel like a swim?" The inspector asked her. "Looks like fun."

"No thank you, we're not here for fun."

"You can say that again. As cute as some of these… girls look, they are hard-working businesswomen. I overheard two of them talking. One of them said she'd asked a bunch of the richest men on the dating app to send her 5000 Rand to prove that they in truth had all that money… and five of them did."

"That's pretty ruthless. How stupid are these men? What do you have to do for 5000 bucks?" Charlie asked.

The inspector thought for a moment. "If I was a real sugar daddy, I'd…"

"Don't say it!" Charlie stopped him from

describing the services a sugar daddy would expect in his eyes.

"Okay, I won't then, but you do get my drift."

"Unfortunately, I do. Have you come across Mr. Whitehurst, yet?" Charlie asked. "I understand that he is one of the guests. Candace Sedibe's former lover and apparently a regular in these circles."

Lerato had given Charlie a last-minute brief of what she should be looking for at the party.

The notorious David Whitehurst was one of her targets. The case file had been sealed by the court, due to Candace's underage status, so Charlie would try to question him underhand.

"Yes, one of the women introduced me to a David Whitehurst earlier. Came across as a bit of a sleazebag. I'm sure it won't be long before we bump into him again."

"That description fits a lot of men here. Can you introduce me to him?"

"Sure." The inspector put his glass on a table.

"You've read the case file this time, haven't you?" Charlie mocked him.

"I barely had the time." The homicide detective

shrugged. "It's been a busy week… oh what am I saying… it's been a busy month. Like every month."

"I'm sure. It's already been established that the cause of death was poisoning and the coroner…"

"…Jonas."

"Yes, Jonas is going to do paternity tests. I think he's already got some DNA samples. You did know that Candace was pregnant, right?"

"I'm not a complete dodo, you know." Marius Vorster pulled a face.

Charlie had to smile. "Just making sure that we are on the same page."

"I guess we are. So you came by yourself tonight. No doubt because of your special… talent. I hope you know what you're doing. But never mind, I promised Lerato Gwala to keep an eye on you."

"Yes, my special talent… Lerato is busy with some other cases. And thanks for keeping an eye on me…"

"Hi, stranger." A seductive voice said and Yolanda, one of the girls Charlie had met here before, walked up to them.

Her dress did not leave much to the imagination

and her makeup gave her face a mask-like character. "You left so abruptly that I had to come and see what you're up to."

She was flirting outrageously with the police inspector and straightened his shirt collar for him, completely ignoring Charlie.

"I meant to come back. Have you met Charlie?"

"Yes, we've met," Yolanda gave Charlie a side-long glance from under rather long eyelashes. Her tone dropped at least an octave only to quickly reach flirting level again. "I'm much more fun, I promise."

"I'm sure you are. I'll see you just now by the pool, alright?"

"Alright, don't let me wait too long." She walked away swinging her hips in a provocative way, greeting men left and right as she went.

"That one's trouble. How did you meet her?" Marius Vorster asked.

"Oh, she was here when Lerato and I came to speak to Mr. Matthews. She didn't like me very much then and even less now, it seems. He somehow got it in his head that I should join his little get-together, so Lerato peddled me off as bait, but thanks that you keep an eye on me. I must admit that I'm not altogether comfortable being here after a little hissy fit she threw at the time."

"No wonder. I think it's the green-eyed monster. You're turning more heads."

"I very much doubt that. They probably just see me as fresh meat. Lerato would be the real man-magnet, but she can't be here. So you have to put up with me, I'm afraid." They sauntered past a couple dancing close-up to the music.

"Whatever you say, Ms Proudfoot. I've been trying to get some info, but everybody seems to clam up when it comes to the murders."

"Maybe I'll have more luck," Charlie said and gave an elderly man with a walking stick an alluring smile. The man smiled back but was immediately distracted by the laughter of his female companion.

"I don't like playing the part of a potential sugar daddy very much, but a few people here have already met Johan Phaladi. Nobody knows I'm with the police, apart from Mr. Matthews of course."

"You're playing your part rather well, I must say," Charlie winked at him.

"Thanks, I guess. Some of these girls look too young to be here and they drink on top of it, but I have to act as if it's okay. Grrr."

They walked around the pool and the girls in the pool eyed Marius. He looked good in high-end beige cargo pants and a short-sleeved white shirt. Simple but chic.

The inspector was aware of the attention as he nodded to a man, leaning casually against one of the tall lamp poles by the pool. The man nodded back. So this was the backup Marius Vorster had brought with him.

What he couldn't see was that Candace had joined the party. A forlorn shape on a low wall by the back stairs, who watched the revelry by the pool from her vantage point in the darkness.

Charlie stopped walking. "I don't want to freak you out, but I must see someone special over there - by myself."

"Are you talking about spirits?" The inspector asked in a low voice. "You can speak to them?" He stared intently in the direction Charlie had indicated.

Charlie said nothing.

"No way - you can actually do that?" The inspector's jaw dropped. "Come on…"

"I didn't say that, but I'm picking things up that other people don't. So let's just keep walking around the pool a little longer. I'll have a look at the party from a different perspective just now."

"Well, I think I'll re-join Yolanda and her posse then, and ask them a few questions about David Whitehurst. Can I get you something else to drink?"

"No thank you, Marius. But you could take this glass from me." He took the empty champagne glass. "Let's get to work. That's what we're here for."

"Yes, let's do that." She checked if Candace was still there. She was.

"By the way, my sergeant is over there by the lamp post, speaking to a woman in sensible shoes. He's here for backup, just so you know."

"Thanks, I figured as much. What about the woman?"

"She must be one of the guests."

"Well, I'm feeling well-protected all the same."

"Good, that's the idea. See you later." Marius Vorster sauntered back on the other side of the pool and paused by a group of chatting men and women. Yolanda touched his arm and acted all delighted to see him again.

Meanwhile, Charlie Proudfoot walked towards the low wall, where the vaporous spectre of Candace Sedibe had settled, when she picked up a conversation that stopped her in her tracks.

"No, I promise you I'm South African, but I grew up in New York…"

Charlie didn't hear the rest of the sentence. She knew that excited young voice and the giggle that followed. Knew both extremely well.

She was instantly distracted and when she looked over to the low wall again, the faint shape that had been sitting there just moments before was gone. She changed direction back towards the floodlit pool area, followed the familiar voice.

And, true enough, there she was in a cute dress with her hair done up and a little makeup. It was Leleti, her little sister, chatting to a short, stocky man, whose bald spot at the back of his head was his most remarkable feature.

Next to her was Emma, flirting with another one of

Eugene Matthews' guests. The man was well-dressed and had a kind, smiling expression, but he was possibly in his mid-forties. The golden Rolex on his wrist spoke volumes.

Leleti caught sight of Charlie and her eyes grew as big as saucers. She stopped in mid-sentence and the man she'd been talking to, followed her gaze.

Was another male making advances at this delightful young sugar baby?

He turned around with an annoyed expression, fully expecting to see one of his competitors approach. Instead, he saw another sugar baby in a red mini dress. Not bad either…

"Charlie," Leleti cried. "What are you doing here?"

"Leti, I could ask you the same thing!" Charlie Proudfoot said, still baffled that her little sister was here. Emma stared past her beau to see who Leleti was talking to.

Next to the professional sugar babies, the two schoolgirls looked like innocent little birds. Emma gave Charlie a little wave.

"Oh hi Leleti's sister," she greeted the approaching

woman. "It's so nice to see you here. Figure that… you were also invited to this party! Leti said you have to work tonight, but now you are also here." She giggled. Were the girls tipsy?

"Well, in a manner of speaking…" Charlie tried to control her voice. "What did you have to drink?"

"Just some juice…"

"Juice, hmm." Charlie smelled the glass. "That's more than just juice."

Leleti looked confused. "That's what I asked for."

It wouldn't do any good to give the girls a talking-to. "I thought you guys were going to a braai with your grandfather. Why are you not with him?"

"Oh, but we are. This is the garden party he told us about. Pretty cool, but no braai…" Emma started to explain, but Charlie interrupted her.

"Where is he?"

"Oh, I don't know. He was here just now… probably got himself something to drink," Emma trilled. "He was talking to a few people over there. Grandpa knows a lot of people here." She pointed to the veranda, where a little group of men acquainted themselves with the beautiful talent.

"You don't say," Charlie said as calmly as possible.

Everybody was drinking champagne or mixers, toasting to each other, but there was no sign of Emma's grandfather.

"How did you get here?" Leleti asked Charlie again. "I thought you had to work tonight."

"I am working…" Charlie smiled at the people around them.

"You are?"

"Can I get you something to drink, sweetie?" The man Leleti had been talking to, asked Charlie.

Of course, she is working, he thought. All the females here were working, and this enthralling sugar baby had now caught *his* eye. Might have more experience than the younger one, which could mean more fun for him.

Charlie was seething by now, knowing full well that she couldn't drop her cover.

It took her a moment to pull herself together. This new situation complicated things.

The balance between work and wanting to protect her little sister was not an easy one to strike, and she couldn't risk making a scene.

"David Whitehurst, by the way," the annoying man introduced himself.

The very man she'd wanted to speak to!

"My name is Charlie, nice to meet you." She switched gears quickly.

"So… can I get you something to drink?"

"Yes, thank you. I'll have a dry Martini, please," she answered and smiled sweetly, as difficult as it was. "Charlie Proudfoot. Nice to meet you." She let him kiss her outstretched hand. The man gave her an engaging smile and tottered off to get Charlie the cocktail she'd asked for.

"Can I talk to you for a second?" Charlie pulled her sister aside. They walked over to a garden bench, where two people were making out.

The couple jumped up when they saw the two women approach and disappeared down the driveway.

"Leleti Clarice Morake, what are you thinking?" Charlie flew at her sister. "You can't be at a party like this!"

"What, why not? I'm seventeen and it's perfectly

fine to go to a party."

"Not this kind of party, girl!" Charlie tried to say in a fairly calm voice. "A young woman was murdered here a couple of days ago and I'm investigating. I have to be undercover to find out who did it – and don't you dare tell anyone. None of these guys here are friends of Emma's grandpa, they are sugar daddies."

"Sugar what?" Leleti said in a loud voice and some of the people nearby were laughing. Charlie looked around and acted as if Leleti had made a joke.

"No really, not that much sugar!" She laughed and gestured, rolling her eyes. The people around them bought the lie and lost interest. Charlie shot her sister a stern look and whispered: "Keep it down. This is serious."

"You said somebody was murdered?" Leleti whispered. She started processing what Charlie had told her.

"Yes. Are you listening now?" Charlie whispered back. "I'm investigating undercover and there's police here."

Leleti stared at her open-mouthed. "You're right.

We shouldn't be here."

"I'm glad the penny is dropping," Charlie said. "We have to get you home. At the very least you need to stop drinking and flirting with these men. The guy you've been talking to is one of the suspects."

Her sister's eyes became even larger. She placed the tumbler she'd been holding onto the soft dewy grass next to the bench. Why was she feeling a little dizzy now? Maybe her sister's concerns weren't so baseless after all.

Marius Vorster had been watching Charlie from the corner of his eye. Odd - why was she not talking to a ghost in the shadows, but a young girl, who seemed very much alive? Did she know the girl? He became aware of the tense interchange.

"Excuse me," he apologised, much to Yolanda's dismay, and hurried over to join the sisters at the other end of the swimming pool.

"Hi, how are you doing?" He greeted them. "Everything alright here?"

"Why wouldn't it be?" Leleti snarled at him. "Sugar daddy!"

"How much did you have to drink?" Charlie

looked straight into Leleti's eyes.

"I told you, I only had fruit juice. Two glasses." Her speech became slightly slurred. "I asked for juice. You know I don't drink."

Charlie didn't believe it for a minute. She must have drunk a mixer.

"Keep it down… Breathe on me!" She ordered her sister. Leleti breathed obediently into Charlie's face. "Young lady! How much did you have to drink?"

"I only had some fruit juice – I swear."

The police inspector touched Charlie's arm. "Will you tell me *now* what's going on here?" His voice had an insistent undertone.

"Hey, don't touch my sister." Leleti glared at him.

"It's okay, Leti, he's with me," Charlie whispered and the girl's eyes lit up.

"I knew it! You have a new boyfriend!"

"Keep it down! And no, not like that…" Charlie Proudfoot turned to the inspector. "Marius, this is my sister. Leleti Morake." She saw his surprise. "I was adopted. And so was Jono. She has no idea what kind of party this is."

"And Daniel... he was also adopted," the teenager

piped up.

"What is she doing here?" The inspector asked softly.

"She arrived from New York yesterday and is staying with her friend Emma's grandparents for a few days," Charlie pointed to the young girl in jeans and striped top, who didn't fit in either, her fresh face virtually free of makeup. "The girls are staying with Emma's grandparents in Roodepoort. Her grandfather told them they were going to a garden party, a braai. She has no idea what sugar babies are."

"I see. That's a mess!"

"That doesn't even begin to describe it. Ooh, I'm so angry."

"Yes, but we have a job to do. I'll take the girls into the house and ask my sergeant to stay with them. Then we mingle some more and…"

"There you are, ladies," David Whitehurst had returned with the cocktail, Charlie had asked him to fetch. When he saw Marius Vorster, he was less delighted.

"Oh you again," he mumbled and handed Charlie the glass.

"Thank you so much," Charlie tried to smile.

"I'll be out of your hair now," the inspector said. "Just give me a moment."

Mr. Whitehurst nodded curtly. That guy was trying his luck with both girls. He knew his kind. Good-looking rich guys had more success with the girls than men like him. He had to somehow up his game…

"Any news?" Marius Vorster asked without giving any of the facts away.

"News? Oh you mean… no nothing yet," Charlie answered unruffled.

"Okay. I think you better come with me, young lady," he addressed Leleti and the two of them walked over to Emma, whose beau had also gone to get her another *fruit juice*. David Whitehurst didn't even try to stop them, but he would hang onto this Charlie he was growing fond of.

Marius took the teenagers into the house.

"We'll organise some coffee for the two of you. The last time I checked, underage drinking was still against the law. Then we'll look for this grandfather of yours."

"He's police…" Leleti whispered into her friend's ear and put a finger on her mouth. Emma swallowed her surprise. This party was not what she'd expected.

"Will my grandpa get into trouble?" She asked meekly.

"I'll have to speak to him first, won't I?" Marius Vorster said. "Let's go."

None of the guests seemed to have noticed anything untoward. Everybody was chatting and laughing and a couple tried out a few drunken dance steps to the song Havana that was playing.

"Some guys have all the luck," David Whitehurst said and watched the police inspector walk away with the two girls.

"Yes, they really do," Charlie said and her face hurt from all the smiling. She wanted to strangle the guy, who had given her sister juice laced with alcohol.

Instead, she flirted with him and said: "but here we are. You can talk to me." She waved her glass around with no intention of drinking the contents. "Tell me… did you hear about the murder of the young woman in the park? I was thinking of not coming tonight…"

She engaged the man in some small talk and it didn't take her long to find out that David Whitehurst had not even been in town for a week, but on business in Durban. He'd heard about the wretched news on the car radio.

And he didn't seem sad about Candace Sedibe's demise at all.

Chapter SEVEN

"Here you are." The guy, who'd sized Charlie up by the cars strutted towards them, holding two glasses. "Hi, David. What are you drinking, Tequila Sunrise?"

The man inspected David Whitehurst's drink. "That blonde young lady I was just talking to seems to have left me for greener pastures."

"Can't blame her for that, Harvey." The two men cackled.

Charlie had the information she needed. There was no need to hang around these two any longer. "Thank you so much for the chat, David," Charlie purred. She turned a little and saw Leleti disappear into the house after Emma and Marius. "I just want to say hello to a friend over there."

"A friend hey? Ah well, the competition doesn't sleep." David Whitehurst walked away in a huff, dialling a number on his cell phone. Charlie stared after him in disbelief.

"Is he always this rude?"

"Don't take it the wrong way," the man called Harvey told her. "He hasn't been laid for a week. Not a bad time to make a move on him if you know what I mean. He has bags of money. Or I could make you a very happy lady, instead."

He winked at her. Charlie was distracted and ignored his remarks.

"Yes… excuse me. It was nice meeting you, but I have to go." She felt like being anywhere else but here, talking to this rich old geezer. Perhaps she should follow Marius and the girls into the house…

"I guess it's not my day…"

Candace was nowhere to be seen. *Oh well*, Charlie thought when she felt a light tap on her shoulder. She turned around and looked at Candace's blurry features.

She was surprised. This was the first time a ghost had touched her. The touch was soft and cool.

"Everything alright?" Harvey asked her. "If you feel chilly, we can go inside and have something to eat or perhaps go to a restaurant. I know a nice place in Bryanston…"

"No, no, everything's fine. I really need to speak to my friend over there," Charlie gave him a charming smile and walked towards the dimly lit area at the back. She knew that Candace was sitting on the low wall as before. She felt an intense pull. What did the murdered girl want from her?

"Are you here?" She whispered and got a mighty fright.

"There is nobody here in the dark." Harvey, the smoker, had followed Charlie. "Now, who's being rude?" His hawkish voice cut through the tranquillity of the place.

His mood had changed in a flash. "What's wrong with me today that all the girls walk away?" He grabbed her arm, seemingly annoyed.

"What are you doing? Let go of me," Charlie raised her voice and tried to pull away from the man's grasp.

"I've paid a fair amount to meet nice ladies at this party…" he started to complain. "But you are not being very nice, are you?"

They heard steps in the dark and the man dropped his hand. Charlie rubbed her arm and glowered at him in irritation.

"Ah, there you are!" The policeman, inspector Vorster had brought along as reinforcement, approached them.

Charlie clicked immediately. "Hi darling, I was just talking to this *gentleman* here."

"Oh, I'm sorry. I didn't know…" Harvey stuttered. "I didn't mean to pester you…"

"Well, three's a crowd." The policeman addressed the unpleasant guy firmly and rolled his eyes at him. "If you don't mind."

"Just my luck," Harvey mumbled and retreated, throwing his arms up in the air as he went.

"Everything okay, madam?" The well-dressed policeman asked.

"Yes, thank you for coming to my rescue. He was getting a bit frisky."

"I could see that. Not the best company I would say."

"They are all very rich guys, can you believe it?"

"I can, madam. We call them blessers. It's not easy to watch what's going on here. But if you are alright on your own, I'll go back now. The inspector asked me to keep an eye on the two girls inside the house, while he's working."

"Blessers… that's too nice a word. Thank you so much. I'll be there just now."

"Take care." The policeman nodded and returned to the swimming pool area.

Charlie waited by herself for a while then she whispered again. "Are you still around? The coast is clear."

Perhaps there was something important Candace wanted to communicate. Would she talk to her at last? A wisp of white smoke rose up on the low wall and took on the outline of the murdered girl.

"There you are." Charlie felt relief. Now she might learn something important.

But instead of hearing words or seeing gestures, she saw the mist forming the shape of a book. A pinkish book with a unicorn on the front. A diary as far as she could tell.

"Are you showing me a diary?" She asked into the darkness and instantly knew that she had guessed right.

"Who are you talking to?"

Charlie Proudfoot recognised the voice as that of Yolanda, who had been so rude to her. What did she want? Marius thought she was jealous, so better be careful.

Charlie had to think on her feet. "Nothing, I'm not talking to anyone. Just thinking aloud," she said. "I do that sometimes."

"No wonder, at your age it must be getting difficult to stay with it." The cocky young woman replied with a snarl.

"What the hell is your problem with me?" Charlie flared up. "Just stay away and do your thing, whatever that is."

She tried to get past the insolent woman.

Yolanda's blonde hair extensions and the short snakeskin dress didn't look quite as garrish in the soft light, but there was nothing soft about that sugar baby.

"If you think you can just get it on with the guys here, you are sorely mistaken. This is my territory. I say what goes and I have first dibs. Understood?"

"Oh, I understand perfectly," Charlie said and pushed past Yolanda. She had no time to quarrel. "Be my guest."

She left Yolanda standing open-mouthed in the

shadows and teetered on her high heels along the paving next to the swimming pool.

The brightly-lit area felt safer to her than being alone with the disgruntled young woman in a dark corner of the property. Here at least, she was among people. Many of the male guests had paired up with pretty girls, dancing up a storm, emboldened by alcoholic drinks.

Her shoes bothered her. This was the longest she'd ever worn them and the hard leather at the back was chafing her heels. She took them off and walked barefoot through the open glass front of the house.

As she entered, Charlie saw the girls sitting on a long cream-coloured couch, their feet on a matching ottoman, holding cups of coffee in their laps.

The policeman was not far away and nodded to her as she passed him. The two were clearly in good hands, but where was the police inspector? Was he looking for the playboy grandfather?

"I'm not feeling so good." Leleti moaned a little when her older sister sat down. "I can't believe there was alcohol in my juice."

"Yeah well, you live and learn. Just keep sipping

the coffee, it'll help you clear your head," Charlie said. "Must I feed it to you?"

She tickled Leleti's chin.

Leleti tried to smile. "Thank you very much, I'm not three years old."

"Thank God for that."

"I want to go home," Emma grumbled. "It's not a very nice party. Grandpa has strange friends. There are not even boys here and the girls are so slutty. How boring. I'm not going to dance with one of those old guys."

"One good thing," Charlie answered softly. "Have you seen your grandpa?"

"No, but the handsome man who was with you, went to look for him. He told me he'd be right back," Emma said.

"He's her boyfriend…" Leleti whispered.

"No, he isn't," Charlie said, "but I know him and he tends to keep his word. If he says he'll come back then he'll come back. So don't *you* go looking for your grandpa yourself, Emma. I'm sure he'll find him. He's good at finding people."

Charlie stood up. "I'll be right back, guys. Don't

you go anywhere."

She walked up to the well-dressed police sergeant. "I'm going to the bathroom," she said and he nodded in agreement.

Charlie didn't need the bathroom - again. She just wanted to use the opportunity to see if she could find the diary, Candace had shown her, upstairs in the room with the baby cot.

She left her heels next to the couch. It would be much easier without them. On her way to the stairs, she picked up a couple of tiny sandwiches at the snack bar. No need to starve herself, just because she was doing some sleuth work for Lerato.

Bertha Lekota, the housekeeper, chatted to her for a couple of minutes, while she inspected the snacks. Bertha took a few plates with leftovers to the kitchen and Charlie stuffed the sandwiches into her mouth, followed by two fried prawns.

Not bad, she thought, *the paying guests are getting their money's worth.*

Still chewing, she wiped her greasy fingers on a serviette as she made her way up to the second floor.

At the top of the stairs, the rooms on the right were

cordoned off with police tape. The CSI team was probably still looking for evidence that could explain what had happened in the TV room the other night. It didn't matter, because Candace's room was down the passage to the left.

The lights in the passage were turned off, but it was probably better not to switch them on and draw attention to herself.

Charlie felt her way along the wall in the near dark, found the door open and slid into the room that Candace had occupied.

It wasn't completely dark in there, because some light from the pool area filtered through the Venetian blinds. The music sounded muted up here, but the party downstairs was in full swing and the guests were clearly enjoying themselves.

She listened out for any noises to make sure that nobody had followed her.

Her foot touched the bedframe and something guided her down to the floor. Okay, so that would save her some time if she didn't have to search the entire room. She padded the floor under the bed and only turned up a lonely slipper.

Now under the mattress. *Not a very original place,* Charlie thought and kept looking. There was still the option to search on the other side of the bed or behind the headboard, but it had seemed to her that she should be looking right where she was. The diary with the unicorn must have information in it that could be crucial to their investigation, so she would try and find it.

Charlie lifted the mattress a little and felt the space underneath. Nothing. She moved closer to the bottom end of the bed. She stopped abruptly when she heard a rustling sound coming from the en-suite bathroom at the back.

Somebody else was here!

She ducked low. The bathroom door creaked. Charlie peeked a little to see who was there. A woman stole into the room and moved swiftly towards the door to the passage.

She had not seen Charlie, who knelt beside the bed and ducked now even lower. There was a possibility that it was one of the sugar babies. Had she also been looking for something – the diary, maybe?

Yolanda was showing an unwelcome interest in

her. Somehow, she got it in her head that Charlie was trying to steal clients from her or unseat her as the queen bee in the house.

What if Yolanda had followed her unnoticed? She couldn't take the chance and accost her to find out. What if it wasn't her and she was dangerous?

They were investigating a murder and murder was not a game.

If she could just catch a glimpse of her... Charlie's hand touched the pointy corner of a flat hardcover book just as the woman sneaked out of the room. For a second, Charlie looked down and when she looked up again, she was gone!

"Gamoto," she mumbled the Greek swear word her mother had used so often when Charlie had been a toddler.

She pulled the book out from under the mattress. Charlie couldn't see much in the dark room, so she held it up against the window. The front cover was a pinkish colour and printed with a unicorn. Just as Candace had shown her with the help of the vapour.

There was no doubt in her mind that this was the diary Candace wanted her to find, but now she'd missed the chance to see who else had been searching the room.

Maybe if she hurried up, she could still find out! But by the time she had scrambled to her feet and checked the dark passage, the woman had disappeared.

Charlie let the book slide into her handbag. What now? Candace might give her some advice, but the ghost was also elusive. Should she go downstairs, phone Jono and ask him to come and take her, Leleti and Emma home? But then she sighed deeply.

There was also Emma's randy grandfather to be dealt with.

Charlie felt anger rise up inside her again. How could this man bring two teenaged girls to a place that swarmed with Romeos, just to leave them to their own devices? He should know better. And that, after he'd promised at the airport to look after Leleti.

As despicable as this was, she had to at least tell him that the girls would not be going back with him to Roodepoort tonight. Not over her dead body… so to speak.

And then there was also Lerato. She couldn't let

her friend down. The murder case was another priority. She should find Marius Vorster and compare notes with him, then deal with the grandfather, then take the girls home. In that order.

Yes, that's what she would do. Charlie groped her way back to the stairs and surveyed the ground floor.

The police sergeant, who had so gallantly rescued her from a very persistent gigolo, stood watching a group of dancers outside on the lawn. He probably wished to be one of the partygoers, twirling around a pretty lady himself.

It had turned out to be a rather big party and not just a small get-together that Eugene Matthews had hosted the night when Candace Sedibe and Nomsa, the cleaning lady, had lost their lives.

Who would be cleaning up tonight after all the guests had left? She wondered. There was no shortage of casual labour in Johannesburg, but the fact that there was a party at all after these tragic events, didn't sit right with her. She took a deep breath, ready to execute her plan.

But then something unexpected happened.

Chapter EIGHT

A loud scream rent through the relaxed party mood and caught the unsuspecting guests by surprise. A series of muffled screams followed as something fell to the ground, then the sound of hysterical crying. It was plainly a woman's voice.

Charlie tried to see what was going on from her vantage point at the top of the stairs. There seemed to be some kind of commotion on the ground floor below the staircase.

She hurried down, clutching her bag with the diary in it. People filed into the hall from the pool area, curious like her what may have caused the disturbance. Some of the men moved to the fore to investigate as if to gallantly protect the women, who stayed closer to the entrance.

The woman, who had screamed could now be heard sobbing uncontrollably.

"Where is Eugene?" A man in a pretentious sports shirt asked, but nobody seemed to know. Then someone pushed a flap door to the private area open and walked into the lower ground passage. The sobbing noises softened and after a moment's silence, the man called out for someone to phone the police or security.

"It's Eugene, I think he's dead."

Jackson, the security guard, who had been standing by the main gate, was rushed in and yelled fiercely into his walkie-talkie. The spell was broken. Suddenly, chaos ensued and many of the guests were on their cell phones, reporting the incident. One of the couples, who'd been in the process of leaving, quickly made their way to the car. Then another.

Leleti – the instinctive thought dashed through Charlie's mind, *is she safe*?

After bumping into a suspicious figure on the second floor, it was better to keep an eye on her. She had last seen her sister on the cream-coloured lounge suite, trying to sober up with a cup of coffee.

Perhaps, Marius had found Emma's grandfather, they had left and Leleti was on her own.

The backup policeman was nowhere to be seen. He'd very likely gone to investigate the alleged dead body. So where was Marius?

Charlie went to the open-plan lounge to make sure that nothing had happened to Emma and Leleti. She saw Emma still sitting on the couch clutching her coffee cup, looking somewhat confused by all the hubbub.

"Emma, where is Leleti? I left you guys only a few minutes ago."

"I don't know, Leleti's sister. I fell asleep. Then there was so much noise and I woke up."

"And Leleti. where was she?"

"I don't know. She wasn't here." She gave Charlie a fearful look.

"That noise isn't about her, is it?"

"No, apparently something happened to our host, but nobody said what exactly. I'm just worried that Leleti left with somebody else."

"Oh no, she wouldn't do that. I want to go home."

"We'll talk about that later. Maybe Leleti's somewhere here in the crowd. Where is Inspector Vorster?"

"Inspector?" Emma's eyes grew large.

Of course, she hadn't told her about Marius Vorster's real identity. "Mhm yes, my friend, who wanted to find your Grandpa, remember?"

"Oh, you mean your boyfriend. He's over there. Just came out of that door."

Emma pointed to the wooden flap door. Of course, it was his duty to get a situation like this under control. More guests were leaving.

"Open the gate!" Somebody barked frantically. "Where is the remote?"

"There's the security from the gate…" Hands were pointing towards Jackson, who stared anxiously at the crowd.

"Nobody's leaving the premises until I say so!" A booming voice ordered. "Find a place to sit down and wait until we ask you questions." Marius Vorster was indeed attempting to get the chaos under control.

"Why are the police so fast today? When my house was robbed, it took you guys 4 hours to come…" Somebody else shouted, but Marius interrupted him with just the right amount of authority.

"Wrong unit, Meneer." The inspector held up his police identification. "Inspector Vorster, Homicide." A panicked murmuring arose. "Please stay calm. There is no reason to panic. We are at a private party, that's all. My colleagues will be here any minute."

"Sure they will," another voice piped up and people started to laugh. "As long as you're not with the Narcs!" The remark drew laughter.

"Homicide? What are you doing here?" another man wanted to know.

"We're investigating a murder, nothing to do with this party."

"Oh, thank God! Wait… what murder?"

"Open the newspaper, man! And it's all over the internet."

"That's right," Marius boomed. "Remain calm, please. We just want to ask you a few questions. Our host, Mr. Matthews seems to have been… injured just now. If you've seen or heard anything, please come forward." A couple of people walked up to him. "Everybody else - sit down, until you've been processed. Please. If you leave, we know who you are."

More murmuring ensued and the mostly barked interplay continued for a few more minutes until sirens could be heard approaching.

"The ambulance is here. Please make space for the paramedics! Give them some space!" The policeman, who'd been with Marius Vorster yelled and the party guests cleared the access from the glass entrance to the flap door. Three paramedics hurried inside with a stretcher and doctor's kits.

The tense atmosphere in the mansion eased a little.

The police inspector followed them inside the passage. "Leo, you're in charge here." It was not easy to get things under control, and despite Leo's best efforts, some of the patrons made for the hills, for whatever reasons.

Obviously, her police escorts had more pressing matters to deal with than looking after intoxicated teenagers. Charlie didn't have a choice but to stay with Emma on the elegant couch and observe what was happening around her.

Most of the guests sat down on the carpet or went outside to find seats in the garden and on loungers by the pool. Leo was talking to two entitled men, who insisted that they had to get home RIGHT NOW.

"Please, sir, sir…"

"The inconvenience… I'm leaving for Paris tomorrow morning. My wife will be up in arms if she knew…"

"Sorry sir, no exceptions. Inspector Vorster will let you know…"

Emma sipped her coffee and stared in fascination at the scene. Her girlfriends in New York would be so impressed that she'd been invited to a party like that. This was Hollywood-level stuff!

"Your boyfriend is so cool!" The girl turned her head and gave Charlie an admiring look.

"He's not my boyfriend… just a friend. What did Leleti say when you saw her last?" Charlie asked the teenager nervously.

"I… I don't know. That… that the coffee was very strong and gave her a headache," Emma stuttered. "I think…" It was clear that the girl hadn't quite sobered up yet.

"That sounds like her," Charlie said kindly. "She told me the same thing before I went to the bathroom."

"I'm sorry, I must have fallen asleep after that. I didn't see where she was going. Do you think something happened to her?"

"No, of course not. I don't know, honey."

"Oh good." Emma finished her coffee. "Can I have

some more?"

"Oh darling, I don't know…"

The flap door opened and the paramedics pushed the stretcher into the hall and towards the entrance.

That could only mean that Eugene Matthews was still alive and had been stabilised. One of them held up a plastic bag with an infusion line going into his arm and tried to keep in step with her colleagues.

Marius Vorster appeared at the flap door and some of the guests got up to ask him questions. A pale Yolanda and Babsie followed him.

There was no trace of Davina. This was evidently not how the sugar babies had expected the evening to end.

"Will he survive?" "Did he have a heart attack?"

The inspector couldn't give them detailed answers only that their host would be taken to hospital and was in a stable condition for now.

He saw Charlie and Emma sitting on the long couch and strode towards them.

"There you are." Emma was visibly relieved.

"I'm afraid, we have to talk later about the case, Ms Proudfoot." He sounded quite formal and surveyed the scene. "Where's your sister?"

"That's a good question. I went to the ladies room and when I came back she was gone." Charlie tried to sound less worried than she was. "I hear that Emma's grandfather has also still AWOL…"

"Yes, well, now that you mention it… I was looking for him when I heard the scream," Marius Vorster said.

"I need to go and find Leti now, Marius. I'm responsible for her. I just hope to God that she didn't go with one of those, those…"

The two men, who had followed the inspector to the sitting area, pricked their ears.

"… gentlemen," Charlie finished her sentence.

The eaves-dropping men relaxed. The last thing they needed at a time like this was the truth.

"Alright. Here's what we're going to do: I'll start processing the guests while you go look for your sister. Then we'll meet here again. If I see her outside, I'll let you know. Do you have your cell phone with you, young lady?" He addressed Emma and the girl nodded. "Good. You come with me."

"Yes okay," Emma said obediently and gave him a

flattering look. "I'm feeling much better now."

"Great," Charlie said. "I'll be back with Leleti in no time. Thank you, Marius."

"Let me know if you need me," he said and Emma followed him outside.

Charlie started her search in the hall, but Leleti was not here. Then she went inside the passage, where Mr. Matthews had been found. Silicon gloves lay in a crumpled heap by the wall and an empty glass vial on top.

She checked in the bathroom to the left, but the door was locked. She knocked on the door and listened, but all she could hear was soft moaning.

A door to the right was locked and straight ahead was the kitchen.

Bertha stood by the massive counter in the middle of the kitchen and Mavis, the cook, leaned against the granite top opposite her, crying with racking sobs. The man in the yellow sports shirt was also there.

"Oh, oh, I just found him like that - lying there. He's dead, he's dead!" Mavis sobbed. "What will become of us?"

"He's not dead," the man in the sports shirt said.

He was a dentist and had been listening to Eugene Matthews' heartbeat before the paramedics arrived.

They barely noticed Charlie and she walked away from the scene, her thoughts racing. She could talk to them later. Right now she had to find Leleti.

The passage curved around the the kitchen and then to the right, where it continued along a glass wall. She knocked on the first door and opened it, interrupting a couple in the process of getting dressed.

The man was Emma's grandfather, but Charlie acted as if she hadn't noticed. They had enough problems and she didn't want to speak to the man. At least, now she knew where he'd been all this time.

"Sorry, wrong room," she said curtly and closed the door. *I'll deal with you later!* She thought angrily.

Charlie continued her search, but the other rooms were empty. At the end of the passage, another staircase led up to the first floor, but there was no sign of Leleti.

Her sister shouldn't have come here in the first place. The girl was still buzzed and god knows who she was talking to right now! She began to feel overwhelmed.

"Candace, I need some help here. Where is she?" Charlie hissed and looked around, but there was no answer or apparition of any kind.

I'm stuck in a nightmare! She thought in despair, then she had an epiphany. *Call Jono!* This situation called for family support. She dialled his number on her cell phone. 'Jono, I can't find her,' she sobbed.

'What? Who? Should I come and fetch you?' Her brother asked. He sounded confused; unsure what to say. 'Is everything okay with you?'

'No, Leti is here… or she was… with her friend Emma. The grandfather's a lech… they didn't go to a braai, they came here and now I can't find her. Just come, please!' She swallowed and pulled herself together, not to start crying outright.

'What? Leti is …what?!' Jono began to catch on.

'No time to explain. Just come please!' She begged her brother.

'Okay calm down! I'll be there just now.' She could hear Jono swear before he hung up. Charlie tried to breathe. What a big mess everything had suddenly turned into! All she was supposed to do was talk to people at the party and find out from the spirit of the dead girl, what had happened that fateful night of her murder.

And now this!

At least she had something to show for it. She touched the diary through her bag.

Sirens blared in the distance, coming closer. This had to be the police. She hastened back to the kitchen. Mavis or Bertha might have seen her!

Charlie found Mavis on her own. Bertha and the sport shirt guy had left. The cook put dishes away into an open cupboard. Platters with food and dirty dishes were scattered around the vast counter top space between them and the large open dishwasher was still releasing steam.

"Oh madam, I didn't hear you come in," Mavis said and quickly closed the cupboard door. She had stopped crying and was working busily. "Would you like something?" Mavis smiled at Charlie, who gaped at Candace Sedibe's apparition sitting on the counter behind the cook. Candace looked terribly sad.

"I'm sorry to disturb you… I'm looking for my sister, Leti."

She saw that the woman was wearing a pin with

the symbol of a popular South African church on her collar. "I was wondering if she came in here."

"You mean the young ladies, who asked for coffee earlier with the nice gentleman. Aye madam, they are too young to drink at a party. Others too. You must not bring them to such a place. It doesn't end well." She was undoubtedly referring to the murder of Candace Sedibe just a few days ago.

"Yes that's them, and I didn't bring the girls here. Emma's grandfather did..." She stopped herself, realising that telling Mavis the story wasn't leading anywhere. "So did you see her again after you made coffee for them?"

"No, I didn't see your sister, but her black friend was in the kitchen to get some sugar. Very polite young lady, but why does she have an American accent? Eish, these young people today, watching American movies all the time."

Leleti loved sugar. She must have asked for it before Charlie had gone to see her and Emma in the living room because Leleti had been drinking her coffee without complaining about the taste.

"I see, thank you. She has good manners." Charlie

didn't correct her wrong assumption about the girls' American accent. Of course, Mavis also thought that Emma was Charlie's sister.

Nothing unusual about that and Charlie didn't feel like clearing up the facts.

What was unusual, though, was the fact that Mavis seemed cool, calm and collected, while all hell was breaking loose just outside her kitchen. Hadn't she witnessed the collapse of her employer?

"She didn't feel very well. I could see that." She gestured with her hand around her face and grimaced. "A child shouldn't be drinking at a party."

"Right. She shouldn't be here at all. Aren't you worried about what's going on outside? Mr. Matthews is on his way to the hospital and the party has all but ended."

"Oh... I'd only be in the way. Bertha went to look when somebody screamed. Poor Mr. Matthews. She always takes care of things around here."

Charlie Proudfoot noticed an array of dark glass bottles lined up under the wall cupboard closest to the dishwasher.

"Emm – yes, but maybe you want to see for

yourself. Two murders and now this… it seems a bit much. What is in these bottles, Mavis?" Charlie pointed to the dark glass bottles.

Mavis looked a bit surprised at her question and moved in front of the bottles in a protective gesture, but the ghost of Candace Sedibe kept pointing to them.

"Oh, they are just Mr. Matthews' vitamins. He takes a handful of supplements every evening. Multivitamins, Q10, milk thistle – things like that."

Charlie didn't let it go. "Do you think it works? Milk thistle, interesting, what's that?"

"It's for your liver, I think. Very good. Muti would be better if you ask me."

"Muti?"

"Traditional medicine. All these modern vitamins are just hokus pokus."

"Yes, I know muti, but that's not the same as vitamins, is it?"

"No it's not the same."

The cook was not in a talkative mood, it seemed. Was Charlie wasting her time?

"Would you say that Mr. Matthews is a good

boss?" She didn't know why she'd just asked this question. The words had simply slipped out.

Mavis Motseke had to think for a moment. The question had obviously taken her by surprise.

"Oh madam, you are asking many questions. Like the other day. Yes, yes I think he pays us well."

The answer didn't quite match the question, but Charlie Proudfoot didn't have time to dwell on it. She needed to find her sister, everything else, the police could take care of.

"I'll be on my way then..."

"Good luck, madam. I hope you find the little one," the cook answered and wiped the fancy kitchen counter.

"Well, she's a teenager. Not so little."

"Still very young." Mavis turned around and began to empty the dishwasher.

"Yes, I agree," Charlie said and whispered, "Thanks for nothing, Candace…"

She left and made her way around the crowd outside the kitchen door in the passage. The conversations she picked up were agitated. Emma still sat on the couch, where she had left her. Next to her sat her grandfather. He tried to convince her of something, but the girl kept shaking her head.

Charlie took a deep breath and joined them in the sitting room.

"You!" She charged at the elderly man. "Don't think for a second that I don't know what you were doing in the room over there!"

"I'm sorry." The grandfather seemed remorseful. "You are Leleti's adopted sister, aren't you?" He didn't look at her.

"You're damn right, I am. We met at the airport." Charlie began to move into gear. "What did you bring the girls to this party for? That you are into sugar babies is one thing, but Emma and Leleti were drinking and flirting with older men and there was a murder in the house just a few days ago. Is that what you call responsible behaviour?"

"But why are you here?" The man had obviously not expected her reaction.

"That's none of your damn business. Not for the same reasons the others are." The grandfather stared at her, then down at the carpet and let Charlie load it over him. "I'm taking the girls with me. My brother is on his way. Yes, Leleti's gone missing, while you were busy with somebody else."

"Why is everybody so upset? Surely not because of me…"

"Your friend Mr. Matthews collapsed outside the kitchen and is on his way to the hospital. In case you slept through it. So I guess the party is over."

He gave her a defiant look. "My wife will kill me if I come home without the girls. I just wanted to be the cool grandpa. I should have kept an eye on them about the alcohol, though."

"You think?! And what about looking out for them? God knows where my sister ended up. She could be in danger or be somewhere, vomiting her heart out."

He stood up. "You are right. I'll help you find her. Please don't judge me too harshly. You don't know what it's like. We've been married for 38 years. I just wanted…" He gave her a pitiful look.

"Charlie?" Jono walked through the open glass doors. "Everything alright?"

"Oh thank God, Jono, you're here. I've been looking for her everywhere on this floor and then…"

Jono caught sight of Emma and her grandfather standing by the couch.

"What the hell is going on here? How could you bring the girls to this party? And why did I see an ambulance coming from this place? Is it Leleti? Did something happen to her?" He snapped at the man.

"Sorry. I was just going to help your sister find the girl," the old man muttered.

Jono turned to face Charlie. "So you haven't found her yet?"

"No, listen to me," she said urgently. "They took the host, Mr. Matthews to hospital. He collapsed outside the kitchen and things have been chaotic ever since. Marius and…" Her cell phone rang.

"Oh thank God…I mean I hope Mr. Matthews is alright," Jono stammered.

Charlie nodded and answered her phone. 'Hello. Yes, Marius… that would be great. No, not yet. Jono just arrived. Maybe we could do that… yes, thank you.'

"Did they find her? I swear if anything happened to my sister you're in trouble, man," Jono was not over his anger yet. The old man stared at his feet.

"No, they didn't. Marius says that police

constables are starting to question the party guests and he could help us look for her."

"Where could she be? And what about me?" Emma asked. I want to come with you…" She shook her grandfather's hand off her arm and gave him a disdainful look.

"Emma, let's go home to Grandma. She'll be worried," he tried to convince her.

"It's up to you, Emma, but it would be better if you came home with us," Jono said

"I'm not going to leave without Leleti." Emma was adamant and Charlie felt proud that her sister chose her friend well, however objectionable the family may be.

Emma's grandfather shrugged his shoulders. "Whatever you say."

"Okay, where do we start?" Marius came towards them. When he saw the old man standing next to Emma, he knew instantly who he was and addressed him. "So you are the elusive grandfather? We've been trying to find you for a while."

The man nodded remorsefully. This evening had not panned out the way he had imagined. "I'm afraid so. I was kind of… busy. And who are you?"

"My name is inspector Vorster, Homicide… Hilda," the inspector called one of the constables over. "Has this man been questioned yet?"

"Not by me," the policewoman said.

"Then he's your next customer. He also brought two under-aged girls to the party and they ended up drunk. Neglect of parental oversight, underage drinking… you know the drill."

"Alright, come with me, sir," the policewoman said and walked away. The grandfather stumbled after her.

Emma had been watching the exchange between the adults in wide-eyed wonder. Although the effects of two glasses of *juice*, the sugar daddies had organised for her, were slowly wearing off, the girl seemed not entirely sure that all of this was real.

She was lucid enough to understand why they weren't supposed to be at a party like this and that her grandfather had crossed some line.

"I don't like this party," the teenager grumbled. "Let me come with you. I don't want to stay here by myself."

Chapter NINE

Emma's big blue eyes begged them not to leave her behind, but they couldn't take care of two drunken teenagers at the same time.

"Emma, the best thing you can do now is to stay here and wait for us, while we look for Leti," Charlie said as calmly as possible. Damn her grandfather. He could have taken the girl home, but that was no longer an option.

"Again? It's so boring. Why can't I come with you?" She whined.

Inspector Vorster noted how her grown-up manner made way for the petulant child again and took a mental note to give his teenaged daughter a call again soon.

"Look, it's more important that we find Leleti than you being bored," he said.

"Why? I could help you find her."

"Because it's safer if you stay in a place, so we know where you are," he explained. "Look, it's safe;

there's police everywhere if you need anything. You could read a magazine…" He pointed to a few travel magazines on the coffee table.

"If I must…" Emma sat down again and began playing with her cell phone.

Marius Vorster turned to Jono and Charlie. "Okay, so where do we start?"

"I already checked on this floor," Charlie informed him.

"Alright, so we start with the first floor. Then the top floor. I believe there is also a cellar below the kitchen. Leo's in the picture. He's putting out a BOLO for your sister, just in case, she left the property with someone or on her own. One of the constables can search the garden and the grounds."

"Could she have gone with someone?" Jono asked in a bewildered tone.

"Unlikely, but you never know…" The police inspector answered.

"What's a BOLO?" Charlie asked. She was not yet familiar with police-speak.

"A search… short for *be on the lookout*. If she is spotted by a patrol car, we'll be notified immediately," the inspector explained. "We'll find her even if she left the premises. Emma's already given me a description of what she was wearing. I didn't have a close look at her, I must admit."

Charlie was impressed. Marius had pulled all of this off, while she'd been searching the ground floor?

"What if she was kidnapped? Some maniac is still on the loose. We have to do something." Jono was beginning to lose his cool.

"Jono, get a grip, please. We'll find her and she'll be okay," Charlie said calmly and hugged her brother.

"Okay, then we have a plan," Inspector Vorster concluded. "Let's not lose any more time and go upstairs."

The three of them clambered up the steps.

"Gee, this place is so big. Where do we go first?" Jono asked. "That side's so dark." He pointed to the passage on the left.

"There are bedrooms and bathrooms that way, from what I remember. You can turn the light switch on." Charlie left out the part where she'd taken what could be called *evidence* because the police would probably have to confiscate the diary and they'd lose valuable clues.

She wasn't sure how these things worked between private detectives and the police and Lerato wasn't here to tell her about it.

Candace had shown her the diary for a reason and she would take care of it.

"Are we allowed to go in there?" She pointed to the police tape on the right. That's where Candace Sedibe was last seen in the TV room."

"I think CSI are still busy with the place." Marius gave the tape a fleeting glance.

"There's another smaller swimming pool on the veranda off the living room. The TV room is separated by folding doors. That's where everybody was when Candace disappeared."

"What, everybody just fell asleep and then she was suddenly gone?" Jono asked.

"Well, pretty much," Charlie answered. "But we're not going to figure that one out now. Let's look if Leti's on that floor, then we can worry about the case again."

"You seem to know your way around this place, Ms Proudfoot," Marius said.

"A little. As I said, I was here before when we first questioned the people in the manor a few days ago and then again when I used the bathroom." Had he noticed that something about her story was off? But he let it slide.

Charlie pointed to the left. "Candace's room is the first one on the left. The one with the baby's crib. I haven't been beyond that room, but we better get going."

"Then let's split up. I'll check out the rooms and the two of you can search the cordoned-off area." Jono walked away, on a mission.

"Okay." Charlie and the inspector turned the other way and stopped in front of the police tape. The yellow tape was intact at the top, but at the bottom, someone had broken the flimsy barrier.

"Well, I never!" The inspector said.

They took care not to break the tape even further and climbed one after the other through the gap. Charlie pulled her leg toward herself and stood up. "What if she's fallen into the swimming pool?" Charlie's voice trembled.

The inspector strode across the carpets to check

through the closed sliding doors. "The lights in the pool are on, but there's nobody out here," he said and Charlie relaxed.

They both noticed a reflection in the glass doors and turned around. There was a dim light in the TV room. The sight made Charlie's skin crawl. The light hadn't been there before.

"That's strange," she said. "There was no light when I used the bathroom up here earlier." They were whispering now.

"You were up here earlier?" The inspector looked surprised.

Charlie nodded and pointed to the passage. "Yes, there's a guest toilet that way."

She felt bad for not telling Marius the truth about her search for the diary in Candace's room, but it couldn't be helped.

What if the woman was in the TV room? What if she was armed? The creepy feeling persisted. What if the woman had Leleti?

"That's strange. We need to check it out," Marius said.

Charlie nodded in silence and Inspector Vorster

motioned for her to stay behind him.

He drew his weapon and held it up when they made their way across the thick carpets into the informal lounge area and towards the softly illuminated room, stopping behind one of the large settees when they heard a sound.

A rasping breathing sound.

Charlie put her hand on the inspector's arm and pointed to the wooden sliding door facing them. It was half-open. An arm in a light blue sleeve protruded from the edge of the couch that faced the flat-screen television.

The arm belonged to a young woman; that much was clear.

All these thoughts were racing through her mind.

Was she in the throes of death? Was she gasping for air?

Oh no, not another body! Charlie thought. She shivered at the terrifying thought as they moved closer to the folding door. Ever so slowly.

Charlie's heart sank.

Were they about to stumble onto another crime scene? Was the scene covered in blood? She couldn't tell. The blood-red colour of the Persian carpet probably concealed bloodstains.

The mere thought of it made her hair stand on end. She suppressed a sob and tried her best to pull herself together.

The arm of the young woman didn't move at all. Was she drugged?

Then another terrifying thought: did the arm belong to her baby sister? For the life of her, Charlie could not remember what Leleti was wearing when they'd run into each other tonight. A dress. Definitely a dress…

The rasping sound was unnerving. At least it meant that the woman wasn't dead yet. A sudden grunt made Charlie jump. Was the victim choking on blood or did a perpetrator press his hands around her neck?

Marius put a soothing hand on her arm.

They were still standing behind the large sofa in the sitting room, waiting for the right moment to go in. Marius Vorster decided not to charge into the TV room and startle a possible perp into doing something really bad.

He was now holding his weapon at the ready, arms outstretched. If the perpetrator was still in there, this might cause an ugly confrontation.

He motioned for Charlie to stay behind the wall next to the opening, peeked inside and quickly surveyed the situation.

The next second he had entered the TV room. Charlie listened and expected a heated exchange, but all she could hear was the rasping sound that had drawn their attention to the location of the victim. That could only mean that the perpetrator was no longer in there.

They had to act fast if they wanted to save the victim. Charlie hesitated. She really didn't want to see a body right now. Or ever again. She just wanted to find her sister.

The seconds that followed were the longest seconds of Charlie's life. What if the victim was Leleti? Unthinkable. *Dear God, I can't lose her as well!* She thought with intent. Then she heard something odd, other than the rasping gasps.

Charlie heard male voices in a seemingly amicable conversation.

Was the inspector trying to calm the criminal down? A psychopath, perhaps. This would be understandable after everything that had happened.

She could wait no longer.

Throwing all caution to the wind, Charlie entered the room and could barely process the sight that presented itself. Marius Vorster stood behind the couch and spoke to none other than - her brother Jono!

Jono was sitting next to the woman on the couch, covered in a powder blue throw. It was Leleti and she seemed to be sleeping.

At least she hoped that Leleti was only sleeping. Nobody tried to stop her when Charlie dashed forward and knelt on the carpet next to the sleeping teenager. She began to stroke her head.

"Is she alright?" Charlie could barely see for tears and felt Jono's hand on her shoulder. She didn't know if she should be happy or distressed.

"She's fine, Charlie," her brother said. "I already checked. Probably just had too much to drink and passed out on the couch. Sounds like her sinuses are blocked, though."

That's what the rasping sound was. Just blocked sinuses. Leleti was snoring. Charlie's brain had to catch up.

"How did she get up here?" Jono wanted to know. "Probably one of life's many mysteries…"

"Oh, Leti!" Charlie kissed her sister's hand. "I thought… I thought…" She lifted the light blue throw. There was no blood and no injury. Nothing wrong at all! Yes, it made sense now…

Leleti's print dress was crumpled and Charlie would never forget the colour. A dusty pink. It was a beautiful dusty pink paisley print.

"I know," Jono said. "So did I at first, but there is nothing else wrong with her. Just a blocked nose."

"Oh thank God!" Charlie felt very emotional. Anything could have happened to her sister. "How did you get in here? I thought you wanted to check out the rooms along the passage!" She looked Jono straight in the eye. "I'm so glad you are here," she cried and knew she didn't make sense.

Her brother leaned against the backrest and took a deep breath.

"I turned around and saw the weapon in Marius'

hand," he explained. "Then I followed you guys. Those carpets are great. I couldn't even hear my own tread."

Charlie looked down on the thick Persian carpet atop the wall to wall floor covering. Yes, it did absorb noise a great deal.

"I stayed in the shadow and went in through the other sliding door, you see..." He pointed to the corner of the TV room, where they had interviewed house guests and staff only a few days ago. "I thought if something is going on inside there, I'd stop it before you do. Call me a hero, but it was just an instinctive reaction."

Charlie looked up and tears began to run down her face. "You tried to protect me? Oh Jono, you're the best older brother ever."

"Oh come on, Charlie, everything's alright." Jono tried to play it cool. He helped his sister to her feet and gave her a hug. She clung to him and felt how her anxiety began to ease.

"She's just had too much alcohol," Jono said. "She'll probably wake up with a hangover and then we move in with coffee and Mom's hangover cure."

"But she's so young… Her first visit to South Africa in ages and then she ends up coming here and this happens!" She sniffled. "She shouldn't even be here."

"She could have gotten drunk at any old party," Marius pointed out.

"Yes, but she doesn't know anybody in Joburg, who'd throw a party like that. And the grandfather promised to look after the girls."

Marius Vorster seemed a little uncomfortable at the sight of the emotional family scene. He needed to stay in tough policeman-mode if he wanted to take charge of the investigation downstairs. There had nearly been a third victim tonight.

"I'm so glad we found your sister. Now if you'll excuse me," he announced. "I'm going to call off the troops outside if you no longer need me in here. I still have two murders and one possible attempted murder to investigate and find answers before something else happens." He put his gun back into the holster and straightened his jacket. "I'll have to go to the hospital as well and see if Mr. Matthews is awake for questioning. Speak to you and Lerato tomorrow."

Charlie nodded. "Yes, of course, we'll speak to you tomorrow," she said and wiped her face with the back of her hand. "Thank you for everything, Marius."

"It's my job. But this whole thing is getting out of hand. I hope we don't have a serial killer on our hands. Anyway, I have to go and get to the bottom of this." He walked towards the door.

"Speak to you tomorrow," Charlie said and looked tenderly at Leleti. The inspector left in silence. Jono picked up the sleeping teenager and carried her to the landing.

"We still have to see if Emma is alright downstairs. Chances are that she's gone home with her grandfather by now."

He carefully transported his little sister to the ground floor behind Charlie. Emma was still in the large living room downstairs where they had left her and looked as relieved as they were when she recognised Leleti in Jono's arms. Many of the guests had already left.

"What happened to her?" Emma asked. "Is she okay? This is such a weird party and now it's over…"

"You can say that again," Jono sighed. "Are you ready to leave?"

"She's just passed out from drinking," Charlie answered her. "That reminds me: where's your grandfather? Do you want me to have another word with him?"

"The policewoman already did. So I told him to go home. Grandma is probably getting worried and I'd rather come with you tonight. Your boyfriend shouted at him as well, because he brought us to the party."

"He's not my…" Charlie tried to set the record straight, but Emma continued to speak. Misunderstandings seemed to be the theme of the night, so she let it slide.

"I thought we were going to a braai, like we do when I come to visit with my parents. But now, there's so much trouble…"

"That's alright. Nothing we can do to change it. I'm sure we'll find a bed for you in the house. How are you feeling? Do you feel nauseous?" Jono questioned her. Emma had also ingested more alcohol than was good for her.

"No, I don't think so. I'm fine. It's not the first

time I've been drinking. We have parties in New York sometimes, you know… "

"No, I didn't know that. You shouldn't drink at all at your age," Jono said.

"We're not that young, you know. And I don't drink as much as some of the other kids do. And I don't do drugs either…"

"I certainly hope so. Is Leti going to those parties with you?" Charlie raised her voice just a little. She knew what those parties could be like. She'd been to a few in the Upper Westside in her time at school in New York.

"Oh no. Leti's too much of a straight arrow for that. I don't think I've ever seen her drinking at any party. Not even when the boy she likes is there."

"What?" Charlie asked alarmed. "What boy?" They stopped walking. The gate was only a few steps away and a policeman, who was guarding it, kept an eye on them.

Jono had parked his car - The Bread - outside in the street, because he couldn't get onto the premises when he'd arrived. What with all the cars parked here already and the two policemen waving for him to drive past.

"Oh, I've already said too much. Leti's going to kill me. She can tell you herself."

Emma pulled a face and Charlie took the girl's hand to guide her along the uneven pavement. Jono and Charlie looked at each other. Oh yes, they would have that discussion with their sister tomorrow.

They spoke to the policeman and Charlie mentioned the inspector's name. He let them pass and they were outside at last.

The policeman stopped a mismatched couple walking behind them, but they had already been questioned and had some kind of paperwork to prove it. Leleti slept through it all, but her friend did not.

"That wasn't a cool party at all," Emma stated for the umpteenth time. "All these strange, old men and not even a braai. No good-looking guys around to dance with. Just boring food and boring music…"

Emma's strong American twang sounded somewhat grating in the near silence. She had lived in New York all her life. Her parents were South African just like the Morakes and had emigrated when Emma was just a baby.

Her father imported South African food items and sold them to shops around the city. He must be making good money to be able to afford a private school. *Emma's parents won't be happy when they learn about tonight*, Charlie thought. Neither would their own parents.

But that was something to worry about later. She had the diary and the girls would be coming home with them. So from that point of view, the evening had ended on a positive note.

"You guys won't be going to a party like that again while you are in Joburg if I have anything to do with it," Charlie said.

"But we're going to have fun, won't we?" Emma yawned. She was slowing down at last.

"Yes, we'll make sure that we will have fun together." Jono shifted Leleti's weight in his arms. "This child is getting heavy."

"She's not so little anymore," Charlie said. "Growing up fast."

They walked down the road under the street lights past the place where the second victim had died such a violent death.

Charlie didn't pay attention to a speck of vapour lingering on the wall where she had first seen the spirit of Nomsa Dube, who'd lost her life in the same night as Candace Sedibe.

It would do no good at all..

Chapter TEN

After the rather eventful evening at the Matthews Mansion, it was hardly surprising that Charlie slept in the following morning.

At home, she had briefly spoken to Lerato and given her an update of what had happened at the party, leaving her friend speechless for once.

She had gone to bed late after tucking the two girls in. That's when Leleti had told her what she could remember before passing out in the mansion's TV room.

'I needed to go to the restroom,' she'd said, 'but the one behind those flappy doors was occupied. I felt nauseous and somebody said there were bathrooms on the first floor. You were talking to someone by the snack table, so I just went up the stairs and threw up in the first bathroom I could find. It was so dark in there and I didn't know where the light switch was. Then I felt tired and I looked for a place to lie down and... I woke up in the car."

'So it was you, who came out of that bathroom!'

'You saw me?' Leleti asked bewildered.

'Yes… well, I was looking for something by the bed. At least I think we were in the same room for a few seconds.'

'I don't know. I can't remember much and I didn't see anyone by the bed. Not that I was looking or anything.'

God knows how she'd been able to find the toilet in the dark, but what were the odds that Charlie had seen somebody else leaving Candace's room. It would also explain why the woman was gone so quickly when she'd tried to run after her.

'Didn't you see the police tape?' Charlie had asked. She had probably gone past the lounge area and entered the TV room through the same door Jono had.

'What police tape?' Leleti couldn't remember ripping the yellow tape that had cordoned off the living area or anything else much, just that she'd fallen asleep somewhere. 'What were you looking for… by the bed?'

'Never mind that. Go to sleep now.'

Thankfully, they hadn't heard from Emma's grandparents until early the next morning. As usual, Jono was the first to get up. He was in the kitchen to make himself a hot cup of tea when the enraged grandmother phoned.

'Yes, I am Emma's grandma. Damn right you are, young man. I nearly had a heart attack when the girls were gone this morning. I always go to bed before 9 o'clock and didn't hear my husband come home last night. Why would you do such a thing? Ron said you just told him you were going to take the children to your house and that he had no choice but to leave without them...'

Jono was surprised to hear the woman yell at him this early in the morning. She had seemed so meek at the airport. He held the phone in his outstretched hand.

'What else did he tell you, ma'am?' He asked.

'What do you mean what else did he tell me? That's what he told me... isn't that enough?' She fumed.

'Did he also tell you what kind of party it was and that he amused himself with a young lady in one of the bedrooms while the - girls – got drunk by the poolside?' Jono tried to say this as calmly as possible.

What he actually wanted to say was: How could you let this scoundrel of a husband of yours take two innocent teenagers to a sleazy party where they get drunk and your husband b**ks some chick, and leaves the girls to themselves?

But he didn't say that. There was no use arguing with this lady.

The sudden silence became louder when she finally began to speak again. 'You are lying, young man. Lying. That's an outrageous thing to say. My husband would never...'

'Oh, but he did. And why would I be at the mansion or the police? You see the police were there because one of the sugar babies and a cleaning lady had been murdered a few days before and the owner...'

The woman interrupted him rudely. 'Sugar what? I'm sure I've never heard of a thing like that. Why would you make up a story and... I'm not feeling so good... Ron, could you hand me the blood pressure pills? Over there...'

The phone call ended very quickly thereafter. Jono had to promise that Emma would phone her grandparents as soon as she woke up.

He tried not to overthink the grandmother's reaction and had just made himself comfortable on the couch. Then, when he began to watch an episode of a hilarious animation series, the phone rang again.

This time, it was Lerato.

He woke Charlie up, handed her the phone and mouthed Lerato before going back to the living room to watch television.

'Yeah?' Charlie yawned.

'What? How come you're not up yet?' Lerato cried cheerfully. 'Didn't the old neighbour-lady have a go at your dogs today?'

'What?' Charlie was too sleepy to comprehend what her friend was talking about. 'Why do you have to yell?

'Am I yelling? Sorry. Your dogs, doll… the new neighbour… her dogs not on a leash…' Lerato repeated telegram-style in a softer voice.

Charlie yawned and rubbed her eyes. 'Oh okay. No, not yet. I think.'

'Wakey, wakey.' Lerato laughed, 'or do you want me to phone back later?'

'No, we can talk,' Charlie grumbled. 'And it's not funny. Now Billie and Popcorn bark every time a car parks in front of their gate and that happens all the time. Customers, I suppose.' Charlie couldn't help but yawn again. "The old woman's probably senile.'

'Yes, okay… Well girl, are you awake, now?'

'Just about…' Charlie put on her slippers. 'Enough to listen to you… what's up?'

'I spoke to Jonas…' Lerato said slowly.

'Who?' Charlie yawned.

'The coroner, remember? The guy who examined Candace's body?'

'Ah yeah, and…?'

'Maybe you should make yourself a strong coffee to help you wake up?' Lerato said. If their conversation carried on like this, it would take all day. 'Did you have too much to drink last night?'

'Not a drop. I'm just tired. The girls on the other hand were plastered…'

'Yes, you told me yesterday. Back to Jonas…"

'The coroner…' Charlie said. She was in the

kitchen now, making herself a cup of rooibos tea, as usual, holding the cell phone pinned between shoulder and ear, while fending off the affections of her excited pooches.

'Very good, Charlie. So he got the DNA results back for the embryo, this morning.'

'Actually, it's called a foetus after the eighth week…' Charlie corrected her.

'Yes okay, foetus then. So apparently, the father is nobody on our list. Not even related or one of her known boyfriends or family.'

'Are you sure? That's odd. Maybe one of her former suitors. David Whitehurst?"

"He was also on our list. And his alibi checks out.'

'That doesn't mean that it couldn't be another suitor.' Charlie's foggy mind began to clear. There had to be an explanation.

'No, it could still be another suitor. That's why I have to find out who else she was in a – relationship – with,' Lerato said. "There's a slim chance that she was raped.'

'Gosh, that so messy! Like an episode of Paternity Court.' Charlie took her cup of tea to the living room and sat down next to Jono. Billie and Popcorn jumped up next to them.

'So that doesn't help with our investigation until we have a positive match.' Lerato sighed in frustration. 'If it's significant at all.'

'I understand.' Charlie sipped her tea and, much to Jono's annoyance, switched the TV off. She put her finger on her lips to indicate that he shouldn't make a noise. 'What else happened or was that all?'

'There's more. Marius phoned me just now. The hospital ran tests on Eugene Matthews and it seems that he ingested poison last night. Not just any old poison, but the same drug that killed our first victim.'

'Nitrobenzene? How strange. The poison that killed Candace. So who would do such a thing and why didn't he die?'

'It wasn't enough to do the job this time. The man's recovering nicely in hospital.'

'What an odd thing to try and poison him at a party. Why?'

'Our inspector spoke to him only about half an hour ago - and - guess what?'

'There's more?'

'We have a prime suspect...' Lerato had been waiting impatiently this whole time to tell Charlie.

'What, a suspect?' Charlie parroted and Jono pulled a face. 'But it can't be Eugene Matthews, I mean he wouldn't try to poison himself...'

'You're rambling, Charlie and no; I'm not talking about Mr. Matthews,' Lerato was itching to tell her friend what she'd found out. 'You'll never guess...'

'Come on, out with it! Gosh, the South African police are more efficient than I thought.'

'No, not because of anything the police did. The suspect contacted me directly, right after I hung up with you last night.'

'Really... and who is it?' Charlie demanded to know.

'Take a wild guess...' Lerato sounded way too chirpy so early in the morning.

'No idea and I have no time to play games. Just tell me already.'

'Mavis, the cook.' There was a triumphant tone in Lerato's voice.

Charlie whistled through her teeth. The dogs sat up and pricked their ears.. 'Mavis, the cook? No way!'

Charlie felt confused. Nothing had been pointing in the cook's direction thus far.

'Yes way!'

'No, I didn't get that from her at all. Candace was in the kitchen last night when I spoke to Mavis. I went to ask her if she'd seen Leleti.'

'The ghost was there and didn't tell you who did it?'

'She seemed more sad than angry. I think the cook truly cared for her. And Mavis seemed happy to work for Mr. Matthews, so where is the motive? She complained when I asked her a few questions because she had work to do and I was holding her up.' Charlie sipped her rooibos tea.

'Okay, work to do doesn't mean that she's innocent. But she basically gave me a confession over the phone. Not just about what happened to Mr. Matthews, but the whole thing.'

'The whole thing?! You mean like killing Candace Sedibe and stringing her up in the park all by herself, then bludgeoning Nomsa Dube to death in the street and now trying to poison her boss? I'm not buying it.'

'Well, that's what she said.' Lerato began to sound

less chirpy.

'A bit far-fetched, don't you think? Maybe she's covering up for someone.'

'That would be a classic one. But for whom?'

'A boyfriend maybe?' Charlie tried to get a feel of what her friend had just said.

'Maybe. Florence did a bit of digging into Mavis' background and you won't believe what she found…'

Charlie's dogs jumped up, ran out and started barking.

'Sorry Lerato, the stupid neighbours seem to be in the street again. I forgot to close the kitchen gate. Jono is going.'

'Those boneheads never take their dogs to the park at the same time…'

'Don't get me started. So what do you wanna do about Mavis? Tell the police to arrest her?'

'Not yet. She said she'd wait for me at the mansion and give me full confession. In writing, if need be.' Lerato sounded excited.

'Do you want me to come?' Charlie asked and finished her tea.

'How quickly can you get dressed? We need to go

together and question her properly, maybe even get a written statement. Then we can also find out, who else our murder victim no.1 was seeing. Two birds with one stone.'

'What about the police?'

'She didn't want me to inform the police just yet,' Lerato said. 'We can talk about it in the car.'

"Emm… I have to speak to Jono. He needs to stay here with the girls. I can't just leave them by themselves. He might have to go to work.'

'Sure. Go and speak to your brother, then get dressed and I'll be there in 15,' Lerato urged her on. The sooner we get there the better.'

Charlie checked her watch. 'Hey, that's not a whole lot of time.'

'Then you better get going, doll.' Click.

Jono promised to stay at home with the girls and Charlie got dressed in record time. He also managed to fill her in about the grandmother's phone call.

"Talk about hypocrisy," she said.

"Acted as if I'd made the whole thing up."

"She'll find out the truth pretty soon. The police took everything down."

While she put eyeliner on, she wondered what could be behind the cook's sudden decision to fess up to murder.

*

When they arrived at the mansion in Ballyclare Drive, no security guard waited at the impressive gate to welcome them. Neither William nor Jackson seemed to be on duty.

The hushed reception was in stark contrast to the lively party mood the day before.

Yesterday, Charlie had walked past a slew of luxury cars and guests on her way to the swimming pool area, and now there was nothing. From what they could see through the gate, there were no cars and no people anywhere.

Lerato rang the bell, but there was no sign of the security guard even then.

"Press the button again. Maybe they are busy talking inside and didn't hear the bell," Charlie said and put her half-empty travel mug in the holder on the dashboard.

Lerato had not lied when she said she'd be there in 15 minutes. So Charlie had grabbed her rooibos tea and a couple of sugar-free biscuits to finish breakfast in the car. She nearly forgot to eat, while listening to the incredible facts that Florence had turned up during her research.

Lerato pressed the bell button again, but nobody answered and the gate didn't swing open. "Should I give Marius a call?" She asked and took out her cell phone. "I don't know what to think of this, but Mavis told me she'd be at the mansion."

"It's probably best to get the police out here," Charlie said.

She looked around, but neither Candace nor the spirit of Nomsa, the cleaning lady, showed themselves to her. Just as Lerato was dialling the inspector's number, the gate opened eerily slowly with a humming sound.

'There we go…' Lerato said unmoved, while talking to Marius Vorster. 'Yes, she practically confessed… yes.' She put him on speakerphone. 'Somebody is opening the gate for us. Not to worry, we're going in now. Let's see what we'll find.'

'I'll be there as soon as I can,' the police inspector said. 'We'll have to take the suspect into custody if her story checks out. At least we have to find out what's going on with her.'

'Should we go in so long?' Lerato asked him.

'You can. Just be careful. You never know what might be waiting for you in there.'

'Alright. Thanks, Marius.' Lerato ended the call. She knew the traffic in town. Marius wouldn't be there anytime soon. "Let's go in."

"Are you sure it's a good idea?" Charlie questioned her decision.

"What?" Lerato asked and drove up the driveway.

"Not to wait for the police."

"I'm pretty sure I can handle a little old lady, Charlie," Lerato chuckled.

"A little old lady who says she murdered two people and tried to kill a third one last night. That's what I'd call a serial killer."

"The police are on their way. They'll probably berate me for wasting their time if she turns out to be a flake." Charlie agreed with her friend. After all that Lerato had told her about Mavis Motseke, it was a definite possibility.

They got out of Lerato's car and walked up to the

back entrance.

Only that this time, there seemed to be an argument underway. Somewhere on the ground floor straight ahead to the left. Two women shouting at each other, but it was impossible to hear what they were arguing about.

As they moved closer, they could hear that the kitchen was the likely location of the noisy quarrel. Lerato went ahead and pushed the wooden flap door open.

The spacious kitchen at the far end of the passage looked like a bright spot at the end of a windowless tunnel. The kitchen door was only open a crack. They made their way forward and could now understand pieces of the conversation.

"Go ka nna botoka... It could be better. We should never have started this whole thing. Never. It was wrong. We have to make it right..." The older woman seemed rather distressed.

"Hi wena! No, Mom... I won't allow it. We need to get you out of here. Mafikeng! Yes… we'll take the bus today. Grandma will hide you," the younger woman cried.

"Oh, you would just run away from all of this? Like a coward?"

"Ee, nka rata jalo." Yes, I would.

"We must make it right. God sees it all."

One of the women, the daughter presumably, gave a disdainful snort. The older woman sounded despondent now.

"Why are you so angry with everybody - with him? He just tried to be kind, to do right by you… no, put that down. Stop this!" There were slapping sounds, then a dull thud and a cry. Something sinister was going on and they were still nowhere near the kitchen.

Lerato gave Charlie a stunned look. "We have to go in!" She drew her weapon and held it so the barrel pointed up. They walked faster.

Of course, they had already figured out, who the two arguing women were.

Florence's research had revealed that Mavis Motseke had grown up in Mafikeng and had three brothers, two of whom had died of undisclosed illnesses in their twenties. Her surviving brother William also lived in Johannesburg. She supported her mother, who still lived in a village close to Mafikeng. She had raised Mavis' illegitimate daughter by the name of Yolanda. Father unknown.

"Goodness!" Charlie didn't have a good feeling about this. "Do I have to go in there with you?" She whispered.

"You can wait outside," Lerato hissed. She threw the door open and pointed her weapon in two directions, before putting her weapon down. It appeared that there was no immediate danger, but Charlie decided to hang back for now.

Yolanda was 22 years old and smart but had dropped out of college in Mafikeng to join her mother at her place of work in the big city. Yes, it was hard to believe, but the cook and the sugar baby at the Matthews mansion were mother and daughter.

Beautiful, short-tempered Yolanda, the girl who had accosted Charlie as a potential rival on more than one occasion. Not a word about their actual relationship this whole time and now they were having a blazing row.

Florence had managed to get the old woman's phone number in Mafikeng through insurance records. Mama Motseke had struggled with her new smartphone at first and dropped it when she answered Florence's call.

She seemed surprised to hear from an old friend of her granddaughter's, who wanted to get back in touch. Yolanda didn't have many friends. But then, she'd been more than happy to supply details of her daughter and granddaughter's life in Johannesburg.

There was movement in the kitchen and Lerato shouted something.

Charlie took a good look inside. A thick rope tied into a noose was lying on the granite counter. Lerato took a few steps back and Yolanda jumped off the counter onto the tiled floor.

She was wearing denim shorts and a simple sleeveless top. Her extensions were tied into a loose knot on top of her head. She took an aggressive stance and picked up a kitchen knife, pointing it at Lerato. Her mother yelled at her in a shrill voice, then there was a sharp clang.

Lerato had knocked the large kitchen knife out of her hand and it had clattered to the tiled floor. At the next glimpse, Charlie saw that Lerato kicked the knife out of reach and grabbed hold of Yolanda and yelled for her to get down on the ground.

"Hands on your back! Hands on your back!" Lerato took out cable ties from her back pocket and tied Yolanda's wrists.

"Please don't hurt her! It's all my fault..." Mavis Motseke cried.

"Yeah, we'll have to talk about that. Won't we? Get up!"

The young woman got up from the ground. Lerato opened the door wide with her foot and pushed her out into the passage. "There, sit down."

Yolanda obeyed. She plunked herself onto the carpet and leaned against the wall. "Charlie, keep an eye on this hothead!"

"Oh, I don't know about that..." Charlie took a step back and gaped at the angry young woman, who glowered in the other direction.

"Can we all go into the kitchen... please?" Charlie begged her friend.

Lerato rolled her eyes and picked Yolanda up by her waistband. "Go sit there!" She pushed her towards two lime-green chairs inside the kitchen.

Charlie gave a sigh of relief and entered the kitchen. Yolanda sat grumpily onto one of the fashionably upholstered chairs.

"What's going on here?" Marius Vorster appeared with two policemen in tow, just as Lerato switched the recording device on. The women looked up.

The inspector saw the noose on the kitchen counter and the knife on the floor. He repeated his question. "

"What's going on with this?"

"I'm so glad to see you," Charlie said. "They were fighting when we got here."

"Yeah, she threatened me with the knife so I had to restrain her. May I introduce: mother and daughter. I was about to talk to Mavis about her statement…"

A bawling Mavis nodded. "We have to make it right. We didn't mean to hurt anyone. You have to believe me."

"Alright. That's why two people are dead and a third is in hospital."

Yolanda didn't say a word, but her mother tried to explain. My daughter can be such a rebel. She would not have hurt the private detective."

"Really? That explains the knife on the floor, but

what about the rope here?" He pointed to the noose.

Mavis began to cry again. "She said she wanted to do to herself what we did to Candace. But the poor girl was already dead and we needed to get rid of the body. We just tried to help Candace, but it didn't work and then…"

"What didn't work?" Lerato asked sharply. The answer to her question had to wait as Bertha Lekota dashed into the kitchen, waving her arms about.

"Come quickly. Come upstairs!" She didn't wait for an answer, turned around and sprinted back along the passage. Pretty fast for a middle-aged housekeeper.

Yolanda just sat in that lime-yellow seat and stared at the ceiling, unmoved by Bertha's plea for them to follow her. In fact, she seemed bored with it all.

"Okay, you stay with her, Khumalo," the inspector ordered one of the policemen and motioned for the other one to come with him. Charlie and Lerato hurried after them.

They all climbed the stairs, turned right and stepped over the police tape that lay in shreds on the tiles.

"Great," Marius Vorster said and was right behind Bertha.

"I don't know if he's still alive. You have to help him, please!" She marched briskly towards the glass doors. Leleti had fallen into a drunken sleep on the other side of the room only last night.

"Who are you talking about?" The inspector shouted the question while trying to keep up with the woman. "What happened here?"

But Bertha was far too upset to answer. The large sliding door to the veranda was wide open and they saw the body of a man floating in the pool facedown.

"It's William! She pushed him in and he can't swim! I also can't swim."

The constable immediately jumped into the swimming pool. The inspector helped him hoist the man over the edge of the basin and started CPR on him. For sure, it was William, the security guard and presumably Mavis' brother – and Yolanda's uncle.

"Who did this?" Lerato pulled on Bertha's arm and the woman turned around. "Who pushed William into the pool?" Surely it couldn't have been his sister.

"It was Yolanda. I heard splashing and came to see

who was in the pool. The police had closed the living room and there was somebody in the pool! William told me. He could hardly breathe and was just splashing around!"

"Yolanda did this? Why would she push him into the pool?" Lerato barked her question. The inspector was pressing his palms rhythmically down on William's chest and continued his mouth-to-mouth efforts.

Mavis appeared in the sliding door and threw her hands up in despair. "William! Ka kopo!" She said a lot in Setswana and ran towards the men working on her brother.

"One, two, three, four…!" Marius Vorster counted and compressed the man's chest again. He put a hollow fist over his mouth and breathed into it twice. Nothing. He repeated the CPR procedure and the man's chest rose.

"Please step back," the inspector gasped. "He's starting to come to." William moved his head and sputtered. Water oozed out of his mouth and nose and he started coughing and breathing noisily.

"Ke a leboga, ke a leboga, sir!" Mavis slumped to

the ground and sat on the wooden deck crying. "Where does she get that evil from? Why did she have to do this?" The woman wailed. Bertha helped her to her feet. "I should have looked after her better when she was a little girl. It's all my fault!"

"Too late for that now," Lerato said drily.

The policeman had been watching from the swimming pool and pushed himself up and jumped out. Marius Vorster sighed with relief and still panting, dialled a number on his cell phone. The number was apparently engaged. He handed the phone to Bertha and said, "Emergency Services. Tell them to send an ambulance."

He got up. "Why would the girl do such a thing?" Marius scolded the cook, who stood with her hands clasped tightly together.

"It's all my fault," she repeated and began sobbing. "Hai matata!"

"Lady, you have some explaining to do!" Lerato said. "We already know that she's you're daughter. What did you do to Candace? Don't you think it's time you told us the truth?"

Chapter ELEVEN

The inspector looked rather surprised when Mavis
Motseke repeated her last statement. He and Lerato
had been questioning Mr. Matthew's cook for the past
half hour and the puzzle pieces began to fall into
place. They decided to go easy on her, as she
reminisced, building up to the current events.

"So let me get this straight: Eugene Matthews is
Yolanda's father?"

"Yes, and I'm her mother. I know it sounds
unbelievable, but it's true. I could not look after her
by myself, and Eugene - Mr. Matthews - did not want
a family after his divorce. It's so long ago, but he
always looked after us…"

They sat in the upstairs living room opposite each
other on the generously proportioned lounge suite.

Nomsa and Candace had joined them as well.
Alas, they were only visible to Charlie, who tried her
best to verify what the cook was saying by vetting
their reactions. Nomsa Dube's spirit was barely there,

a wisp to Charlie's eyes, hovering by one of the Art Deco standing lamps in the room she had kept clean and tidy while still alive. Candace, on the other hand, made eye contact with her every so often and nodded or shook her head.

"I was so very young - so green. We had an affair when he was married to that… bitch!" Mavis spat the word out angrily. "Deborah! All she was after was his money. Going to beauty salons, having brunch with her girlfriends and the boyfriends… hai wena! And she treated me like a slave all day long."

After relating the circumstances of Yolanda's existence, Mavis started telling them how the tragic events had begun to unfold over the past few weeks, but she kept going back to a much happier time in Johannesburg not even 20 years ago.

She looked small in her cook's uniform as she sat squeezed against the armrest of the large couch, her eyes fixed on her hands, feeling the heavy burden of guilt on her shoulders. Charlie sensed that there was more to her story.

Bertha had given the soaking-wet policeman a towel, slacks and a tennis shirt from Mr. Matthews' closet. She'd taken his clothes to the laundry room to wash and dry them, while he'd gone downstairs to the kitchen to make himself a coffee and help watch the unresponsive young woman in the lime green chair.

She had also gone to fetch dry clothes for the gardener, while Mavis was being questioned, and tried to make herself as useful as possible.

A paramedic was seeing to William outside on the deck. He was lying on a pool lounger, holding onto a teacup, trying to get his bearings, while the paramedic knelt next to him. Inside the house, Mavis still spoke to the detectives.

"So you were working for Mr. Matthews back then?" Lerato asked her.

"Yes. I came to work for the madam and she was not nice to him. She was also not nice to me. So we started seeing each other behind Deborah's back. I wasn't sorry about it. She was not a nice woman."

"How did your relationship with him start?"

"He was lonely and I didn't know many people in Hyde Park. He didn't go out much and I was in the house more than his wife. He saw that I was pretty and nice to him. I think he liked that. So we… you know."

Charlie could see Candace sitting on the easy chair now, where she had drunk the poisoned wheatgrass shot. Nomsa was still hovering next to the standing lamp.

"Yes, we can guess. How long did this relationship last?"

"Oh, a while. We had to be careful that Deborah didn't find out. She would have skinned me alive and I needed the job."

"So they got divorced…"

"Yes, after I left. I went to Mafikeng to have the little one. Deborah never asked, who the father was. They got another maid, but she didn't last a month, then another. Eugene sent me money every month. His new business was doing well and he was very generous."

"And then you went back?"

"My mother was looking after the baby and I went back to work in Johannesburg. The witch was no longer there and I was happy when Eugene asked me to come and work for him again. I can cook well and he liked my cooking. Madam had sent me to cooking school…. he had started his new business with Mr. Whitehurst. He said it was like a dating website. Very modern."

"Mr. Whitehurst is a partner in the business?"

"I think so… he was always here. But they could choose any girl they wanted and I was not Eugene's girlfriend anymore. That was fine. I was with him and he was like family to me. The father of my daughter."

"You stayed here, working for him as his cook this whole time?" The inspector probed.

"Yes," Mavis looked up from her hands for just a moment.

"I went back to Joburg when he asked me to come and stay here. He had many girlfriends now… and he had to entertain his business friends, look after the young women, who came to the house. So I cooked and did what I had to do. As long as I could stay close to him."

"So you stayed with him, despite all the girlfriends?" Lerato asked.

"It was not easy, but he looked after me. He gave me money for my mother and for Yolanda. He is good to us. I have a small flat on the top floor and Yolanda came to stay with me last year." Mavis looked up again. "She said it would be easier to find a rich boyfriend, who would look after her. The boys at the college in Mafikeng wanted to go out with Yolanda and it distracted her from her studies. She wanted to become a secretary and her father paid for the school, but then she wanted to come to Joburg. Hai wena!"

"Did she come to visit her father when she was younger?"

"No, he didn't want people to know that he had a child out of wedlock. He kept two pictures of her as a baby. I think my child wanted to know him better, but she didn't know him well."

"Was she angry with him?" Lerato already knew the answer.

"Hai, yes she was angry. He was her father and he gave the other girls more attention than her. Although she is so pretty. Especially Candace was his favourite. 'It's not even his baby she's carrying,' she would say. 'He's always giving her vitamins and health drinks and what not. Treat's her like a jewel. I am here and he doesn't even see me, Yolanda would say."

"That's sad. I understand that she would be angry with her father for showing others more attention than her," Charlie cut in.

"But I never thought she would be *that* angry with him! She was always nice to Candace because she was pregnant. Yolanda knew he wouldn't marry her. The girls talked about finding rich boyfriends together and they fought like sisters. But she would never harm her father. Candace didn't want the baby anymore. They talked about it and Yolanda told me to mix the muti into her drink to help her get rid of the baby." The cook looked at her hands.

"Hold on, back up. So Candace had realised that Eugene Matthews would not marry her and she no longer wanted the baby?"

"He'd given her an engagement ring - but to other girls also, sometimes. He likes to play these games with them. He is like a teenager, not a grown man."

"That's not very kind. Mr. Matthews has already confirmed the story. He calls them promise rings…" Lerato. "No wonder Candace thought they were engaged."

"He didn't want to be mean. He has a good heart. Just… he doesn't want to grow up." Mavis sniffled into her paper tissue. "With all the girls around the house, why should he get married? Yolanda told her that he wouldn't marry her. No way. Better to find another boyfriend."

"But she was pregnant…"

"Yes, Yolanda knew the computer. She looked up how to get rid of a baby. Candace was five months along, so if she wanted to get rid of it, she had to do it quickly. She wrote down the name of some muti and said I should speak to my friend. She is a nurse at the hospital. Yolanda gave me some money and I paid my friend. We didn't want to kill her, but I gave her the poison! It was me."

Mavis Motseke began to cry again, still staring at her hands. Lerato handed her the box with tissues that was on top of a very modern and expensive-looking chest of drawers. The cook took a tissue and noisily blew her nose. There was ever so slight movement by the standing lamp. Nomsa had shifted just a little.

Charlie Proudfoot felt sorry for these tragic women, caught up in the extravagant lifestyle of a middle-aged playboy, who meant so much more to them than they would ever mean to him.

"You mean the nitrobenzene?"

"I think that was the name that Yolanda wrote down. She said it was safe to get rid of the baby and then Candace could have her own life and leave the mansion."

"Did Candace ever tell you, who the father of her baby was?"

"She said it was her stepbrother. Justin. He would come into her room at night, whenever he was staying at home from university over the holidays."

"That explains why all the other matches have come up negative," Lerato sighed. A tear rolled down the cook's cheek and she didn't bother to wipe it away.

"She tried to tell her father, but he was busy and said she should talk to her stepmother if she had a problem. The stepmother was as bad as Eugene's wife. Only thinking of themselves. She told Candace, she must leave the house, because she was a slut and tried to cause trouble for her son."

"Oh my word. And she told everybody else that Candace had run away and was lazy, taking drugs and what not."

"What happened then?" The police inspector asked.

"Candace was crying a lot and said that she wanted to talk to her father, but he doesn't care about her - only his second wife and their children. He would not believe her anyway that the golden boy was doing that… and there was no point. She called him The Golden Boy. Eugene didn't know the whole story. She only told me and Yolanda."

Charlie could feel the confusion and despair the woman exuded. Was it time to tell them about the diary she had taken from Candace's room? There had been no time to study the contents, but she'd told Lerato about it and they would get onto it as soon as they were done here.

Actually, they had to report back to the client, Mr. Sedibe. The policeman had come back upstairs and was outside by the pool taking a statement from William, the gardener. The paramedic left. William would be okay and seemed to be sleeping on the lounger,

"Too much money is not good for people. It makes them not think right," Mavis said with contempt in her voice. "The baby is her stepbrother's, but he doesn't take responsibility. He says he doesn't know if it's his baby."

There it was - the truth. So easily obtained, but they already knew that Candace's stepbrother had not been directly involved in her death. He'd been at university in Grahamstown.

The inspector cleared his throat. "Yes, well, thank you for clearing that up, Ms Motseke. Now let's talk about the night of Candace Sedibe's – death. There was a small get-together and you had your plan to give her the nitrobenzene… then what happened?"

Mavis told them about how she hid the capsules in one of the empty brown vitamin bottles in the kitchen and when she prepared the wheatgrass shots for everyone in the house after the few guests had left, she gave Eugene Matthews, Davina and Babsie just a little bit. It worked. They all fell asleep in their bedrooms.

"We opened three capsules for Candace to make sure it worked, but she started breathing funny and looked so pale."

"You didn't think of taking her to the hospital?"

"I wanted to take her, but Yolanda and Bertha said she would be fine and what would we tell the doctor?"

"So you let her die?"

"I didn't know she was dying. My friend told me you have to take a lot to die, so no more than three."

"Research on nitrobenzene shows that in some cases a lot less than that can be toxic," Charlie revealed. "It's unpredictable. Everybody reacts differently. It's mainly used in dyes and sometimes people even react or get sick from being exposed to it in very small quantities. You could have killed all of them."

"I didn't know. I didn't know…" Mavis Motseke wailed and dabbed her eyes. "We thought it's safe… And Eugene thought they were vitamin capsules on the night of the big party. I forgot to put the bottle away with everything that was going on. Now he's in hospital. It's all my fault."

She hung her head and the tears were dripping onto her neat white apron. Charlie noted that this woman was still in love with her former boyfriend. She didn't mean to harm him or anybody else, but she'd gotten herself into something so big that it had spun out of control very quickly.

"Lucky for you, he's doing better. His stomach

was pumped and they gave him medication. He should make a recovery soon," The inspector said.

"I'm so glad. He's been good to us… we didn't know what to do. Then Bertha came back from her day off."

"Yes, then what happened? Was Bertha Lekota there? She told us she went straight to bed after coming home from visiting her family in Vosloorus," Inspector Vorster pressed on. He still had to take a statement from the daughter and obviously, Bertha Lekota as well.

"I called Bertha when Candace was breathing so fast. We didn't know how to help her. Bertha always takes care of things around here."

"Yes, so what happened next?"

"When we got back to the TV room, Yolanda was sitting on the floor crying and the poor pregnant girl was so pale. There was vomit on the carpet. She said she felt dizzy and couldn't see properly. She was supposed to be sleeping like the others. My friend at the hospital told me that even a little bit makes you sleep. Nomsa was still there and she cleaned up the vomit. She wanted us to go to the hospital, but Bertha said no."

Mavis told them that Candace had tried to get up from the easy chair she was lying on, collapsed and fallen back onto the chair, gasping for air.

First, they thought this was normal and helped her into bed, but the miscarriage didn't want to start. Then she stopped breathing altogether and everybody began to panic. Neither Mavis nor Bertha knew what to do.

According to her testimony, Yolanda had wanted Candace to miscarry and leave the mansion, not die from a nitrobenzene overdose.

They had dabbled in something they didn't know how to handle. But there was no proof that Mavis Motseke was telling them the whole truth. The policeman in Eugene Matthews' clothes was now leaning against the wall by the sliding doors and watched the interview.

"Nomsa was finished cleaning up the vomit and when she saw that Candace was just lying there so still, she starts screaming that we must call the police or an ambulance to save her, but Bertha said it's too late."

Nomsa wasn't so easily convinced and tried to phone emergency services, but they didn't answer.

"Yolanda took away her phone and wants to step on it, but Nomsa jumps on the ground and takes her cell phone. She grabs her bag and runs out. She wants to go to the police station and report the whole thing.

"So Bertha killed Nomsa?" Inspector Vorster asked. Mavis shook her head.

"Not then. We woke up William and he carried Candace to the car. Jackson didn't want to wake up, he was so drunk. Bertha said we must make it look like she killed herself." Mavis Motseke's voice was now barely audible.

"Where did the rope come from?" Lerato wanted to know.

"William had some in the garden shed at the back of the property. He went there with Bertha to look for a shovel or something to dig a hole, but then Bertha sees the rope and they decide to use it instead. It's faster than digging a hole."

"You didn't think for a moment that it might be wrong to do any of that?"

"Sir, I didn't think. It was like my mind was empty."

"What did you do then?"

"Yolanda knows how to drive. I was so sad for the girl. We just wanted to help her get rid of the baby and now she was dead!" Mavis Motseke wiped her eyes with the sleeve of her cook's uniform. "The ancestors had other plans for her. We just wanted to help," she repeated.

"What happened next?"

"Bertha said we could make it look like she committed suicide by hanging, but not here. We have to go to another place with lots of trees like a park. Yolanda knows the way to Emmarentia Dam. So we drove there."

"Could you speak up, please?" The inspector placed the recording device directly in front of her and leaned back again.

"Can I have some water, please?" Mavis' voice was a mere whisper now.

"Sure. Why don't we all go down to the kitchen and continue our conversation there?" The inspector suggested and got up. Lerato took her recording device and walked towards the stairs, followed by Charlie and the policeman, who guided Mavis down to the kitchen.

Yolanda was still sitting in the lime-green chair, sulking while the police constable watched her from behind the counter.

The inspector sent him out to take a break and the Khumalo took his place. Yolanda sat up nervously when she saw her mother enter. The two of them exchanged woeful glances.

"Where were we?" Marius Vorster asked while Charlie prepared a glass of water for the unhappy cook. She spoke up, also for her daughter's sake, who seemed to listen to her account of the events on the fateful night of Candace Sedibe's death.

"We see Nomsa on the corner when we drive to the park." Mavis looked to her daughter for confirmation, but Yolanda stared angrily at the wall.

"How did she get out of the gate and into the street?" Marius Vorster asked.

"Nomsa has a remote. We call her from the car, but she doesn't stop walking."

"She ignored you?"

"Yes. Bertha tells Yolanda to stop the car. They both get out and start arguing with Nomsa. She cries and says it's wrong that God will punish all of us. Yolanda starts pushing Nomsa. Bertha is angry and looks around on the ground. She picks up a stone and when Nomsa starts walking again, she hits her with the rock on the head. Yolanda pushes her and she falls."

"Thanks, Mom…" Yolanda folded her arms more tightly in front of her chest. It was the first time she had spoken since the blustering fight with her mother.

"I have to tell them the truth now, child. God and the ancestors will not forgive us if we don't make it right."

"Sure, whatever. We'll all go to prison, anyway." Yolanda gave Charlie a hateful glance and stared at her mother.

"So you didn't plan to murder Nomsa Dube, then?"

"No, I didn't. She made me so angry," Yolanda replied. "Did she want to destroy all of us? It was an accident! She kept saying that her stupid church does not allow her to say nothing. That it was wrong. But Candace was just supposed to have a miscarriage and we could all go back to our lives. My Dad would want to get to know me better and Candace could go back to her father's house. But Nomsa just wouldn't listen to me and Bertha!"

"It happened too fast," her mother took up the story. "Next thing, Nomsa is lying on the ground. She's bleeding and doesn't move. So we have two dead people. It's too much! My child is a good child, but she has a temper, sir. And Bertha was also angry. We don't want trouble with the police at the house, she said in the car. We put Nomsa in the bushes and forget it happened. Enough to deal with one body. Mr. Eugene doesn't know anything about that. He is feeding us and Nomsa wanted to destroy all of that, Bertha says. I was crying a lot."

"Then you drove to the park?"

"Yes. I don't remember how we got in. Just that William and Bertha put the rope in the tree and I cried even more when I saw that beautiful girl hanging there."

"What did Yolanda do when all of this was going on?"

Her daughter stared at her.

"She was holding me and just went to check and told them to hurry up. What if somebody sees us…"

"Somebody did see you," the inspector said.

"Oh?" Lerato was surprised to hear it. "There was a witness?"

Charlie listened up. "Who's the witness?"

"Park security picked up a hobo this morning and found an expensive ring in his pocket. We checked - it's Candace Sedibe's engagement ring. He didn't want to talk at first, but then he said that some people had hanged the young woman and run away. He only took the ring after they had left. The security guards thought he was lying and took him to the police station. We weren't sure what to think until we found out what ring he'd stolen. I knew that Ms Motseke's confession didn't hold water."

"So he's your only witness?" Lerato asked.

"Yes, so far. We'll offer him a deal to take the theft charges off the table if he gives us a statement and identifies the perpetrators."

"We didn't mean to harm the girl. We wanted to help her, but we did the wrong thing and now God will punish us."

"Why did Yolanda want to hang herself from

the rafters in the kitchen? She doesn't seem very remorseful."

"How… I'm sitting here and you ask my mother…"

"Would you tell me the truth?"

Yolanda looked away in a strop, so her mother answered.

"She does feel bad about Candace, sir. She was afraid that she also has to go to prison and she'd rather die than go to prison so young."

"I see," Inspector Vorster said and switched off his recording device. Lerato did the same with her device and put it in her handbag.

"She must not do anything to herself. Eugene will pay a good lawyer for us. He's family."

"We'll see. Right now, all we need is the truth, Ms Motseke."

"I'm telling you everything, but please… my daughter."

"You should have told the truth from the beginning. It would have made it easier for us to investigate the case and get justice. Now you're both not only guilty of involuntary manslaughter but also lying to the police and obstruction of justice."

"Bertha said that we…"

"Yes well, Bertha was wrong, wasn't she?" Charlie replied vehemently. "Speaking of which… where is Bertha Lekota?"

*

There was no trace of the housekeeper anywhere on the property. She had simply vanished. Today's security tape was examined, while Yolanda, William and Mavis were taken to the police station for their involvement in the deaths of two women and accidental injury to Mr. Matthews.

Police would also pick up the hospital nurse for supplying the illegal distribution of a restricted substance.

The recording showed Bertha Lekota leaving the property on foot with a tog bag about 1 hour ago. It was clear that she was attempting to run from justice.

Not if Inspector Vorster could help it. The police had to react quickly. A BOLO was issued for her arrest and one could only hope that the woman would be picked up in the city or not far from the Matthews mansion. If they waited too long, she could be hiding out in a multitude of places.

Charlie and Lerato left it to the police. They had somewhere to go. There was still the small matter of briefing Walter Sedibe about the facts of his daughter's death.

They stopped at a small shopping centre on the way and sat in a quiet coffee shop and read the diary that might shed some light on Candace's situation.

Her scribbled entries confirmed that Justin, the stepbrother, had gotten her pregnant during the Easter holidays. He'd been obnoxious for a while but made his move when they were alone in the house.

Mr. and Mrs. Sedibe had gone to a celebration at the club with the younger children and were gone for a good few hours. Candace felt ashamed afterwards. Although she'd had quite a few sexual experiences under her belt, Candace was by no means callously promiscuous. And he was her brother!

The young woman's anguish jumped out from the scribbled pages. She started to fiercely refuse the self-involved young man. Then when she discovered that she was pregnant she tried to talk to him.

His cool, disapproval was more than she could bear. He'd suggested that she should get rid of the brat, but none of them had the money for such a step. How Candace Sedibe had tried to speak to her father, then to the stepmother about her pregnancy, spoke volumes.

The entries were often smudged by what looked like dried tears:

The witch doesn't even want to talk about it. She threatened to tell Dad that I was taking drugs and sleeping around if I as much as breathed a word. She's probably doing it anyway. Dad didn't want to speak to me. He said I must go to her. He's busy, I'm going crazy. I feel so alone.

There's no other way: I must leave the house before things get worse. Justin doesn't care. Nobody cares. I'll go to Eugene. I've already told him. What else am I supposed to do? I need somebody on my team. Eugene will help me.

He's a good man and he said that he'd marry me one day. He has feelings for me, different than with the other girls, and he doesn't want another child growing up without a father if he can help it. He was even a little happy when I told him I was pregnant... maybe he'll love the baby when it is here.

Eugene said I can stay until the child is born, but then I have to leave the mansion. The engagement is off. Where am I supposed to go now? I can't go back home.

Daddy will kick me out. The witch is going to see to that. Give the baby up for adoption? No. It's not too late to get rid of it. Many girls do that. They get medicine somehow. Maybe Mavis knows where I can get tablets to do it.

I don't know how he found out. He was disappointed, but not really angry. I apologised to him. He didn't hit me like Justin did. Mavis and Yolanda are the only ones, who know the truth, but they wouldn't tell him. They are my friends... He doesn't want me to get an abortion. I have to think about that.

I asked Yolanda for help today. Yolanda was only too willing to help. I know she's jealous because Eugene likes me. She says that Mavis can organise good muti from her friend, a nurse at the clinic. Drops or capsules that she could put in my drink and they will work and the baby is gone. My problems are gone.

The nurse said to Mavis that they'll make you sleep and a bit sick, but when you want to get rid of the baby, you must take a little bit more. I didn't want to know when they would do it. It was better so. They should think that it was a normal miscarriage. I'm just afraid that something might go wrong, but what choice do I have?

The efforts of the police were to no avail. Bertha Lekota had gone to ground and it would take weeks before the public learned what had happened to Mr. Matthews' housekeeper.

Chapter TWELVE

Walter Sedibe glowered at the pages the two sleuths had put before him. They were copies of the diary entries that described the events leading up to his daughter's disappearance after Easter.

His mind struggled to process what he was reading.

They had buried Candace only yesterday and now it felt as if she was speaking to him again. He finished looking over the last page and sat back with a grunt.

The waitress had just brought their coffees and a rooibos tea and health-sandwich for Charlie.

They'd been sitting in a quiet corner of the coffee shop's veranda in a Bryanston shopping centre for all of 15 minutes.

Lerato had insisted that they should meet on neutral ground and without his wife. The truth behind Candace's death was a delicate matter and the last thing they needed were her stepmother's contemptuous remarks.

"And you are sure that this is what Candace wrote

herself?" The well-dressed man was still in denial about the roles his wife and stepson had played. He was hiding behind a façade of nonchalant indifference, so typical for someone with much wealth and influence.

"We found it in Candace's room at the mansion; under her mattress. There's no doubt in my mind that she was the one who wrote the diary." Lerato tried to be calm, but she didn't have much patience for this obstinate man.

Charlie watched the deceased woman's outline sitting on the railing behind her father. She could feel how desperately she wanted him to show remorse or grief at her lot. Even love, perhaps.

"You should recognise your daughter's handwriting, Mr. Sedibe," Charlie said.

He shot her a withering glance. When debriefing their client, she had omitted the fact that Candace had practically shown her the diary and where to find it.

Not many people would want to listen to a paranormal explanation and Walter Sedibe didn't strike her as somebody in touch with his spiritual side.

After a few minutes of silence, his tough demeanour began to crumble. Memories of the cute little girl with the dimples and cheeky look in her eyes, who resembled his first wife so much, flooded over him.

The man slumped in his chair and could barely hold back his tears.

"I'm so sorry. I didn't know. I never thought…" he mumbled and swallowed only to flare up. "How could she? How could she do this to me?"

"You mean your wife? Well… sometimes people…" Lerato began to console him.

"No, not my wife. Make no mistake, I know who she is," he lectured her. "I didn't marry Edna for her kindness or intelligence. She's tough; knows how to take care of things, how to represent the family and spend money where it matters. We have an image in the community to uphold. My first wife… she was different, but love makes you weak. She made me weak." He swallowed hard and his eyes remained dry. "Candace knew how important it was to me to make a good impression."

The two detectives were taken aback by the gush

of words and his apparent lack of empathy. Clearly, his daughter's death, who had met with a tragic end while trying to find love in all the wrong places, had not managed to melt his heart.

His daughter and grandchild had died and his wife and step-son had had no small part in the drama that led up to their deaths.

"You may keep the copies, Mr. Sedibe," Lerato said in a matter-of-fact voice. "And thank you very much for the final payment. I think we are done here."

"Yes. Yes, of course." The mask of self-control and being-in-charge returned.

Walter Sedibe had narrowly avoided an emotional scene. Unthinkable, to show such weakness in public, where somebody might recognise him. "What about the diary? Isn't it the property of the family?"

"I'm sorry, the diary is evidence."

"Then I trust that the contents are kept confidential." He rolled up the papers and stretched his hand out for a final handshake. "Well, then there is nothing more to be said."

Lerato reluctantly took his hand and Charlie just

nodded her goodbye, while pretending to be busy drinking her rooibos tea.

He nodded and pushed his chair back against the table, leaving his untouched coffee cup to wobble slightly on the porcelain saucer.

"Thank you very much for your work. I will recommend the Maitirelo Agency if one of my acquaintances should be in need of your services."

"Thank you, that's very kind of you," Lerato said politely.

"I sincerely hope that the perpetrators will be dealt with harshly in court."

"Yes, but that's up to the courts to decide. We don't have any influence over matters of this nature."

"Of course," he said curtly. "And I can trust that the press won't find out about the family background?"

"We always stick to our agreements, sir. The police, however, are not bound by our agreement if it has any bearing on the case. Just be aware of that."

The man nodded one last goodbye and walked back into the coffee shop.

"He didn't even pay for his damn coffee," Lerato

complained. "Argh."

"Does it matter? He's out of your hair now."

"Thank goodness for that," Lerato sighed. "Can you believe this man? My dad may not be perfect, but at least he has a heart."

"He's paying for this, believe me, one way or the other."

"Why what is it that you know and I don't?" Lerato asked.

Charlie lowered her voice. "Candace is with him. I saw her hovering like a dark cloud around him as he left. I believe she was eager to hear one loving word from her father, to know that he's on her side for once. Now he'll sit with two unresolved problems for a little while longer." She put down her cup of tea. "I could literally see the change in her… and then there's the little one as well, although much smaller. They are not going to leave him alone for a while."

Lerato's initial shock changed to uneasy mirth. "Perhaps until a sangoma helps him get rid of them," she chuckled. Charlie was not convinced.

"He doesn't strike me as someone, who seeks out the help of a sangoma."

"You never know… but I'm not going to hold my breath." Lerato changed the subject. "What's going on with your sister and her friend? Are they still staying with you after all that drama at the blesser-party?"

"Yes well, Leleti said she's not going back to Roodepoort. She had a hangover of note the next morning. That should put her off parties for a while. She also thinks that the grandparents are hypocrites and she couldn't pretend to be happy to stay with them," Charlie said.

"And Emma?"

"The police opened a case against the grandfather. The girls are still underage. That's all I know and as long as they are safe, I don't really care what happens to that old coot and his phoney wife."

"Yeah, let them stew in the mess they've created." Lerato snorted and finished her coffee. "Can I have a bite of your sandwich? Hmm, looks delicious…"

"Sure, help yourself," Charlie smiled. "Leleti and Emma seem alright. I'm sure they'll bounce back. It's going to be just an interesting story they can tell their school buddies back home. Jono and the girls have worked out a schedule for the rest of the holidays. Things like going to the zoo, a concert, picnics and hiking in the Magaliesberg. I'm told that I have to come to some of them."

"That sounds like fun. I haven't been to the zoo in ages. Have you spoken to Emma's parents yet?"

"I let Jono deal with it, but I think they weren't too happy when he dropped the bomb. Judging by our parents' reaction, the grandparents won't be in for a happy reunion. I mean would you be okay with it if your dad did something like that?"

"Probably not. I guess her parents will have to air some dirty laundry, when they come back from Cape Town."

"Yeah, but until then, we will make the holiday as enjoyable for the girls as we can." Charlie picked up the daily newspaper from a rack between two pillars next to their table. The headline had caught her attention:

SEDIBE MURDER CASE

Mother and Daughter Duo Accused of

Involuntary Manslaughter

Murderous Housekeeper Still on the Run

The subheading promised a juicy story, but the article didn't keep that promise. What they knew about the victim and the circumstances had been rehashed from the previous articles.

The police had not yet released all the information, while the court case was sub judice. The article repeated an interview with a well-known psychologist, who spoke about the problem of blessers zooming in on vulnerable young women in every sphere of society.

Then the article highlighted the devastating number of femicide cases in the country and the incompetence of law enforcement.

All that the reporter had dug up since yesterday was the fact that the police had not been able to track down the fugitive Bertha Lekota at this stage. They were following up on various tip-offs from the public – and there were many. Bertha had not returned to her home in Soweto and her family could not or would not give information on her whereabouts.

"Hopefully, this case blows over soon or I'll stop reading newspapers altogether," Lerato moaned and sipped her coffee. "Why are you not eating your sandwich?"

"Hmm?" Charlie was distracted by the article in the newspaper.

"Alright, I'll order a new sandwich for you," Lerato said and called the waitress over to their table. "Yes, the same one. Thank you."

Charlie was still reading. "They managed to score an interview with Whitehurst," she scoffed. "I met him at the party. What an unpleasant fellow… It says here that he's an investor with the SugarDaddyDateMe website. I wonder how the reporter got hold of him. Until now, he never had anything to do with anything and he knew Candace only in passing. Most misunderstood man in South Africa right now."

"Apart from our former president. I have to go soon. So glad I never have to see Walter Sedibe ever again," Lerato answered and made short shrift of the sandwich she was holding.

"Maybe I should also go home. I'm sure that there was something planned for this afternoon." Charlie vaguely remembered the mention of a picnic in the park.

"You will stay a little while longer," Lerato

ordered her friend.

"Oh, why? We're done with Sedibe …"

"Because you must eat, remember? Blood glucose levels and so on…"

"Yes, okay," Charlie continued to read the front-page article. "Thanks, *mom*."

"And I must get back to the office." Lerato chewed on the last morsel.

"I thought that Andy was supposed to relieve you at the office this week." Charlie looked up. "Isn't that what you said?"

"I know, but his wife feels down and he's helping her with the baby."

"Don't they have family to come and help out? What's going on there? It sounds to me as if Andy is taking advantage of you…" Charlie said annoyed. "That's not fair."

"Don't judge him. He's a softie when it comes to his family."

"I've never even met the guy, but I know that he should pull his weight at the office. It's his business as well."

"I know…"

"Are you coming on the weekend? The girls are so excited to try out the fire pit." Charlie changed the subject. "They've been collecting kindling for days."

"I'll let you know tomorrow. Didn't you ask Marius Vorster to come with his daughter? How old is the kid?" Lerato asked.

"She's 15. He wasn't sure if he could make it, either. Never mind. If you guys are all too busy to come, then our family will have all the fun."

The waitress placed another health sandwich on the table and Lerato pushed the plate right in front of Charlie. "Did she think I was going to eat two sandwiches? Tztztz."

"Thanks for looking after me, Lerato." Charlie folded the newspaper and put it back on the rack. "Alright sandwich, here I come."

*

The middle-aged woman wore her best shweshwe dress today. She had taken extra care as she got ready this morning.

It was a glorious morning and she enjoyed her walk along the footpath between fields of weaving long grass outside the village of Taba Nchu.

The woman was headed for a stand of acacia trees on the other side of the Black Mountain that dominated the landscape of the area. She knew many of the villagers and had waved to them on her way, taking care not to be drawn into lengthy conversations. Not today.

The village was the home of her late husband Robert and the woman was still on good terms with her sister-in-law. It was here that she had spent the happiest years of her life as a young bride.

Her husband had been a kind man and never berated her for not bearing him sons. The two little girls, who looked so much like him, were all grown up now. They had played in these very fields with the other village children and learned how to read and write under the shady tree over there.

Her husband had made a living as a mechanic and also maintained the few agricultural machines and vehicles in the surrounding villages. They'd never had much, but they had been happy.

Then one day, the neighbour's wife had come running to find her. Robert had been in an accident and her life had changed from one day to the next.

They'd had no money for the hospital and her husband had died at home of an infection. The modest funeral came and went and her brother-in-law had taken the house back, small as it was.

He had given her two weeks to plan ahead. Two weeks wasn't much, but her family in Soweto had told her to come. That they would figure things out together. Now she had brought them nothing but shame.

Yesterday, she had spent all day on the bus from Soweto to the Free State. She hadn't visited in a long time and was looking forward to seeing her sister-in-law and smell the long grass in the fields. Remembering the good old days.

During the trip, she'd had much time to reflect on her hopeless situation while watching endless fields and the rolling hills of the Free State moving past.

She had phoned her mother from outside the small supermarket below the room she'd rented in Soweto for a month before packing her few belongings. Then she'd taken the bus to Taba Nchu.

After her husband's death, life had been everything but easy. Then good fortune had led

Bertha to a job that turned things around for her. The girls had done well at school. They had found husbands and jobs, while Bertha worked her way up from being a maid in Killarney to becoming the housekeeper of a very important man in Bryanston. S

he did not have a special love in her life, but Eugene Matthews was good to her and her children were thriving.

Being a god-fearing woman, she had always disapproved of Mr. Matthews' lifestyle, but her life was comfortable and she knew that his comfort guaranteed hers.

Bertha had been working at the mansion for a year when Mavis arrived from Mafikeng and began to take over the kitchen duties for the growing number of visitors that moved through the house.

It had taken Mavis years to open up to Bertha.

At first, she didn't believe that the little girl in the photographs that Mavis had shown her was Eugene Matthews' daughter, but then she had seen the pictures in his bedroom on the third floor.

It was true, he had fathered a child with the woman, who was cooking their meals and catered at the many parties.

Bertha had gone through an inexplicable phase of jealousy, but after a while, she could see that Mavis had no intentions of taking her place in the mansion. They had become friends again and life settled back into a comfortable routine.

She began to forget about Thaba Nchu and Robert and the love they'd once shared. Bertha felt in charge of her destiny again. She'd found a new purpose in life and would be damned if she didn't do her best to keep things the way they were.

Eugene Matthews appreciated her commitment and efficiency as his housekeeper and the above-average salary was another reason to keep her boss happy.

But life changes and life at the mansion changed when Yolanda, the product of Eugene Matthews' and Mavis Motseke's illicit affair, arrived late last year.

Yolanda had the first run-in with a sugar baby in the first week.

Amanda had been the undisputed queen bee at the mansion and regularly accompanied Mr. Matthews on business trips.

She was the poster girl of the SugarDaddyDateMe company, beautiful and smart, but she was no match for Mr. Matthews' daughter.

The following week, it was Yolanda, who went on a business trip with her father – and it would remain the last. Her temper got in the way of closing an important deal in Europe and the next time, it was Candace, who'd accompanied Mr. Matthews.

And that was only the beginning. She decided to become the best-ever sugar baby to win a place in her father's heart, but that hadn't been the right way and her mother steered her towards men who were more serious about relationships.

It had been Yolanda's temper that got in the way on the night Candace had died. They should have reasoned with Nomsa in a way that made sense.

Instead, Bertha had been spurred on by the girl's anger. Her perfect life was in danger, but she should have known better.

At her age, wisdom should have been her advisor, not anger. When she picked up that rock, it had felt as if it was the only way she could save what they had at the mansion; that everything would resolve if Nomsa was no more.

She had not thought about the consequences her actions would have or about Nomsa and her family. Bertha revisited the guilt and shame and grief about the murder she had committed. It was a capital sin. There was no arguing with God. What she had done was unforgivable in the eyes of the Lord.

A herd of cattle grazed in the field to her left. *The herd boy must be around somewhere*, she thought. That's the last thing she needed; that somebody bore witness to what she was about to do.

But the herd boy was nowhere to be seen.

He had probably fallen asleep in the pasture, chewing on a blade of grass, while watching the puffy clouds drift by.

At the next fork, she followed the path closer to the mountain. The rope in her hand felt rough, but she held it tight. Her sister-in-law used it to tie goats and donkeys to posts in the yard.

She had to make friends with the rope that would be her only companion. The first acacia trees came into sight and Bertha breathed in the spicy country air deeply; the scent of warm grass and happiness.

Insects were serenading her as she picked a sturdy branch that hung low enough for her to reach.

May God forgive her for what she was about to do. She knew it was a sin, but she couldn't help herself. There was no hope left and she'd rather end it all here and now, surrounded by the things that had made her so happy - once.

A few hours later, the shepherd boy saw something odd dangling between the acacia trees nearby. Something bright blue was swinging in the light breeze.

He stretched himself and yawned before leaving the herd behind to investigate. The boy was shocked by what he saw. What he didn't see was a small speck of vapour on the rickety fence and it didn't remain there for very long.

Nomsa was leaving now and she was no longer alone.

The End

THE AUTHOR

Evadeen Brickwood grew up with two sisters in Germany and studied cultural sciences and languages. As a young woman, she travelled extensively and many of her books are inspired by her experiences abroad. Feeling adventurous, the newly qualified translator moved to Africa in 1988 and worked for two years as a secretary and language teacher in Botswana. The author eventually settled in South Africa, where she got married and raised two daughters.

In Johannesburg, Evadeen Brickwood studied computers and management of training and worked as a corporate software trainer, professional translator and lecturer at WITS University. In 2003, she began her writing career with youth novels in the 'Remember the Future' series, about adventures in prehistory. Book 1, the award-winning 'Children of the Moon', has been published twice in South Africa and translated into German. The author now self-publishes and you can look forward to the new, off-beat Charlie Proudfoot series, which is set in South Africa.

The author's websites are:

http://www.evadeen.wixsite.com/charlieproudfoot

http://www.evadeen.wixsite.com/novels

http://www.evadeen.wixsite.com/youngbooks

Evadeen is looking forward to your mail and can also be contacted on social media, incl. Facebook, Twitter, Instagram, Pinterest, google+ and Goodreads.

ABOUT THIS EPISODE

Sugar daddies are called blessers in South Africa. Although many of these men are wealthy, entitled and bored with their lives, most blessers are ordinary men who give - often under-age girls - money, cell phones, clothes and food. Most importantly, the give attention where it is in short supply.

When my daughters were in high school, a girl they had been in primary school with, became pregnant by a taxi driver. Let's call her Petronella. Petronella was beautiful and smart, she had her whole life ahead of her – and in desperate need of love and attention. That's exactly what attracted her blesser. Another girl went missing from school, another one from a local shopping centre. They were gone for days and everyone searched or prayed for their safe return. When they eventually showed up again, it turned out that they had gone with blessers. This was only in our community, but the problem is growing.

When I researched sugar babies, I came across young women who make this lifestyle their career choice. Some manage to move on after paying off study fees, other become professional courtesans. Strictly speaking, they are not prostitutes, because sometimes these arrangements involve occasional sex and sometimes it's simple companionship. They accompany wealthy men to events, have dinner with them, go dancing, pose as girlfriends. Their beauty and wit are the goods they sell, so I would call them modern courtesans.

At the time when the idea for this book came together, a beautiful young woman was found hanging from a tree in Kwa-Zulu Natal. Soon. the hunt for her boyfriend was on. The remarkable fact was sadly not that she had been killed by her partner. This raises barely an eyebrow in a country where violence against women and children and femicide has become endemic. The murdered woman had been eight-months pregnant with her boyfriend's child and become an inconvenience. Although the story in the book draws from these events, it is entirely fictional and the two women sleuths are at the centre of the action. You can look forward to the next episode which was inspired by the world of business..

Evadeen Brickwood

THE NEXT EPISODE
in the Charlie Proudfoot Series

4

Judith Holland is overjoyed when she lands a rewarding
position with a large pharmaceutical company.
At last, her sacrifices over the years are paying off. Despite
some bullying from new colleagues, accountant Judith settles
in nicely. When the first employee is found stabbed to death,
rumours start flying. Then more bodies are turning up and the
question on everybody's mind is:
who will be next?

MORE BOOKS BY EVADEEN BRICKWOOD

This adventure mystery tells the story of 22-year-old Bridget Reinhold who is not exactly the adventurous type, but when her sister Claire disappears in Southern Africa, nothing can hold her in England. Bridget launches herself into the search in Botswana and encounters obstacle after obstacle. She learns the basics of the native language and culture and soon moves to the capital city of Gaborone. Soon, her mission is plunged into turmoil as everything seems to be going wrong. Just coincidence or is there something more sinister at work?

Another mystery novel set in modern South Africa. This time, the murders of a ranger and a rare black rhino in the idyllic Shangari Safari Park rattle the local community of Rutgersdrift. Sofia Helenius from Finland lives at the lodge with her boyfriend Tom Rutgers, the owner of Shangari. Sofia is tormented by a secret she yearns to share with Tom, but the cruel events grab the limelight and put everything else in the shade. One of the native Khoi-San families is known to communicate with wild animals, but what if the criminals get wind of this gift?

When another murder happens in the city of Johannesburg, smouldering secrets begin to unravel. How are the murders connected and will it be possible to halt a relentless crime-syndicate in order to save an African paradise?

As if growing up in the seventies wasn't difficult enough, teenager Isabell Bertrand is also too rebellious for her parents' liking. A novel treatment with hypnosis appears to be the perfect remedy and Dr. Albrecht regresses Isabell to her early childhood and even further back. She experiences previous lifetimes and then one in particular: could this beautiful young woman in a silk sari, who was forced to choose between two men, really once have been her? Years later, Isabell is invited to a wedding in Pakistan and memories of a forgotten love come flooding back - with dangerous consequences.

Can you imagine, suddenly living in the past? Not last year or in the Roman Empire, but a really, really long time ago?

Katherine, Trevor and Chryséis embark on a sea voyage and sail across the prehistoric ocean to the remnants of a sunken continent. Suddenly everybody seems to be after a mysterious speaking stone from the fabled land of Lyonesse.

Finding their way back to Alesia and their home in the future, turns out to be more difficult than the time travellers thought. War breaks out in the Mediterranean Sea and forces Katherine, Trevor and Chryséis to flee inland. Nothing here is the way they thought it would be, and who has ever heard of Egypt without pyramids?